The Might Series

Child

Prophesy

The Might Series

Child
Prophesy

W.W. MORSE

W.W. Morse

Published by W.W. Morse, Battle Creek

ISBN-13: 979-8-218-05538-7 (paperback)

ISBN-13: 979-8-218-05539-4 (eBook)

First Edition

Contents

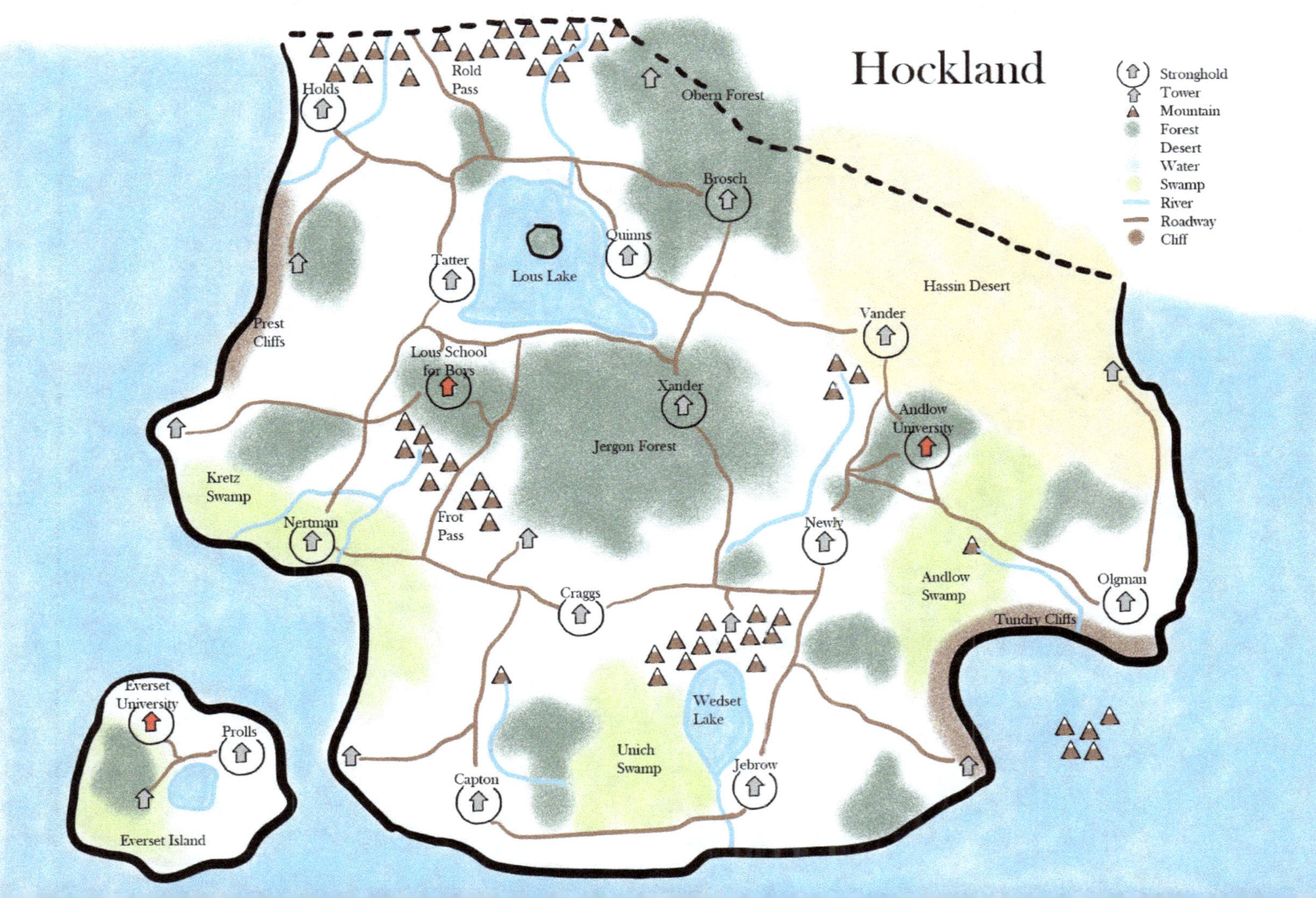

Hockland
Holds
Rold Pass
Obern Forest
Brosch
Quinns
Tatter
Lous Lake
Prest Cliffs
Lous School for Boys
Xander
Vander
Andlow University
Jergon Forest
Kretz Swamp
Nertman
Frot Pass
Newly
Andlow Swamp
Craggs
Olgman
Tundry Cliffs
Hassin Desert
Everset University
Prolls
Unich Swamp
Wedset Lake
Jebrow
Capton
Everset Island
Stronghold
Tower
Mountain
Forest
Desert
Water
Swamp
River
Roadway
Cliff

Prologue

She didn't know where she was and was too scared to say anything. The last time she was crying, they hit her. Her little hands and feet were tied, a blindfold was wrapped around her eyes. She just wanted her mom.

A vision of her mom lying on the floor with her eyes open, her aura gone and pool of red liquid around her body, made her start to whimper. She would never see her warm glow and be in her embrace again. Tears accompanied the girl's whimper.

"Stop that child!" a deep voice said. They were on the move, bumping along for over a week. The men who held her captive did not like her. They at least gave her food and water, sometimes would force her to eat, even though she was too sad at times to do so.

She controlled her whimper, trying her best to stop so she wouldn't be hurt again. A short while later the wagon she was riding in came to a halt. She still had the blindfold on, so she was unsure what time of day it was.

Rough hands grabbed her, and she shrieked. "Settle down now!" that same hoarse voice said to her. "Don't be fussing." She felt the binds loosen from her wrists and ankles. Before she could stand with feeling in her feet again, the blindfold was taken off. Her eyes had to adjust to the sudden light. She shakily stood, blinking, trying to get her eyes to focus.

She was unceremoniously half-dragged, half-carried to a structure that was nestled in the trees. It was a tower, maybe one of the watch towers from the stories her mom used to tell her. These towers were scattered around Hockland to protect the people from invaders. It had been many years since the last raids, long before she was born, and some of these towers crumbled, neglected from use.

The tower she was looking at had not crumbled. It was still standing tall, reaching up over the trees. There was only one door and that was where the cruel man was taking her.

Two men were standing on either side of the door. She guessed that they were guards. They weren't there to guard her from the man whose hand was clamped around her upper arm. Her captor strode up to the door and pushed it opened, not sparing any glance at the two guards. He entered the building with her in tow. It was dark in the tower, only small streams of light from high windows illuminated the space.

They didn't stop once they were inside. The man continued to a stairwell that led down. The farther they went, the darker it got. It started to become harder to see the stairs, but it didn't matter if she did miss a step, with the disgusting man's grip on her, there was no way that she was even going anywhere, let alone fall. She tried that before, escaping, and only received either a beating when she was dragged back or was tied up to unmovable objects.

Finally, they reached the bottom, things scurried in the shadows making her jump. They reached another door were the hinges squeaked as the door was pulled open by the man. She didn't get a chance to take in the room before she was thrown in. She stumbled and held out her arms, so she didn't land on her face.

She heard the door close behind her and a lock engaged. She slowly got to her feet and looked around her. The ceiling was high, seeming like she was in a pit. There was only one small slant of a window toward the top, her only source of light. The rest of the room was bare, shadows that could play tricks on the eyes. She shivered at what could be crawling around in here with her.

She rushed to the door, grabbing the handle, and tugging at it. It wouldn't budge. She didn't want to stay in here. There was no warmth, no life in this room. She couldn't stay in there. Tears began to blur her vision. They couldn't do this to a child.

She started to pound on the door with her little fits. "Let me out!" her little voice broke the silence. "Don't leave me in here!" She pounded on the door until her hands hurt. She sunk to the floor, sobs escaping from her.

It seemed hopeless. She was trapped in this dismal place and there was no one there to help her. Her family was dead, all of them slaughtered by men like the ones that captured her. She had no loved ones that would know that she was gone. She didn't know what Fate had in store for her, but at this moment she did not like her odds.

How much time had passed? Days, months, years? She didn't know. Her whole world was now this black hole. She was given food, but how often she could not tell. Long ago she soiled her clothing, she was not given new ones. She was left in her filth. They didn't care if she lived or died. She had to get used to how she smelled. It would have been nice to get a wet cloth, but the people holding her captive were not kind people.

She stared up at the sliver of light streaming in, it was the only sign of what time of day it was. She knew when it was night because she was in total darkness, unless there was a bright moon, even then it was obscured because of the trees surrounding the tower.

No one came and talked with her. She really was alone. Too frightened of her surroundings, she didn't sleep. She closed her eyes to think about why they would do this to her. What did she do wrong? She hadn't lived long enough to be anybody.

A sense of calm came over her and a vision appeared behind her closed eye lids.

It was the violet sky, twinkling lights, and a great big moon shining down on her. She was traveling, far away from the tower she stayed in. She was surrounded by men, but these men had bright shining auras. Their Spark shined with hope. It was a wonderful feeling, being safe.

That feeling was cut short as soon as her eyes opened. She would not be able to see the sky, day or night, for a long time. Her own Spark was dwindling but this vision poked at that Spark, making it dance with excitement.

Will she be saved some day? She had to hope and believe that what she was shown would come to pass. This dismal place was not her destiny. Her life was in Fate's hands, she just hoped that Fate would continue to give her the strength to be able to believe and hope that this was not her end, but only her beginning.

Chapter 1
The Tower

8 years later…

"How much farther? We should be getting close." Gene Newly was the strategist, except this plan wasn't one he was comfortable with. He and three others decided to scope out Brosch Stronghold. It's been eight years since the Great War. The man behind the reason that their country was divided lived in Obern Forest. Rumor was the stronghold was impenetrable. Gene and his allies were hoping that they could find any way to stop this tyrant.

Penn Holds was walking slightly ahead, leading this party through the woods. They were taking the least direct route to Brosch Stronghold. They were not going to chance it using main roadways, hoping to sneak up to the stronghold on the north side. They were only on a scouting mission and not here to get themselves killed.

"We're getting close, I think." Holds turned his head from side to side, slightly looking around him.

"What do you mean, you think? You're the one leading." That's all they need, to be lost in the woods. Gene looked above him, noticing there was a lot of coverage, making it almost impossible to know the direction they were going, especially now that it was starting to get dark.

"We've been traveling east, and we need to go just a bit more and then turn south," Holds commented.

"Fine, but don't lead us into the next country. I know the woods aren't guarded like they used to be, but I still don't want to give them a reason to invade. We have our own problems to deal with."

They walked for another half hour. The sun was getting close to the horizon, soon it would be dark. Gene was not too fond of the idea of camping in the woods, especially woods this dense and so close to the stronghold.

As the light faded into darkness, Holds stopped abruptly, holding a hand up for the others to do the same. Gene stopped in his tracks, afraid that he would be noticed if he moved even a little bit. Holds moved behind a large grouping of trees and gestured silently that everyone make their way to where he was.

Gene, careful with his steps, tried his best to glide to him without making noise. As soon as he reached the other three, they all huddled close, so they did not raise their voices any louder than a whisper.

"There's something up ahead," Holds said nearly inaudible.

"What? I didn't see anything," Gene said, maybe a little too loud. He wasn't positive.

"I'm not sure. It looked like a building of some kind. We shouldn't have run into anything, right Newly?"

"You are correct. The map we had showed this part of the forest to be vacant, just forest. That's why we picked this route."

"What do we do?" one of the other men asked. Gene tapped his chin, thinking of the best way to handle this.

"We scout it out," he answered. "That's why we are in the area, the better we know what this building is, the more prepared we will be when we come through this area again."

"Sounds good," Holds continued, "we'll each spread out, but keep in sight of each other. We will make little noise as possible. We are not here to be killed, so don't rush in there. If we do, we go on my signal. Got it?" The small group nodded in compliance. "Let's move."

Their small band spread out, Gene going to the left. Once each person was positioned, they moved forward as one, ducking and weaving in and out of the trees and brush, sticking to as many shadows as possible. It was getting easier as they went, since the sun was almost gone behind the horizon.

It didn't take long for Gene to see the outline of the building that Holds had spotted. How could he have missed that? It was huge! It had a large circle base and shot up above the trees. Was this an old watch tower? He hadn't been to this area of the country before so the building could be one of those towers.

If it was one of those, the structure should have been unkempt and crumbling like others he'd seen. However, as Gene came closer, he could see how very opposite that was. The tower was immaculate, with no visible sign of damage. Even the area around the tower seemed to be cleared on a regular basis.

They came up to the edge of the cleared area. Gene was behind a large oak. He leaned around the side to survey the area. What he saw was slightly confusing. It took a few moments to understand what he was looking at.

There seemed to be a door, which had two lit torches on either side, signifying it as the entrance. Two black figures lay on either side of the door. It was hard to tell from this angle, with what little light playing tricks, if the figures were men.

He looked over at Holds to see what he was thinking. Should they move closer to investigate? He found Holds behind a mulberry bush. Once Gene had his attention, he shrugged saying what they should do now. Holds glanced around the bush one last time, deciding the next steps their small crew would take.

Holds signaled for them to continue forward, right into the cleared area where there were no places to hide. So, Gene slid out around the oak and carefully crept forward. The four of them slowing came together toward the door. Each person had a weapon of some sort drawn. Gene had a long hunting knife in his hand. He wasn't going in unprepared.

They reached the down figures, and they were indeed men. Each one stared blankly out, as if their life ended right where they stood. Holds was braver than Gene and he bent down and felt the first man's neck. Then he made his way over to the second man and did the same.

Holds stood back up and looked around to their small band and shook his head. Dead.

Gene stepped forward and bent down to the first man, trying to determine the cause of death. There looked to be no signs of outward damage. No blood pools shone. Nothing except dead, empty eyes.

Holds gave the signal for the other two to make their way around the circumference of the tower. With a gesture toward the door, he and Holds moved to the closed entrance.

Holds squeezed the latch and pushed open the door. They stood in the doorway, both weary of walking into a bad situation. A sweep with his eyes around the interior room showed there was no one. It was lit by a few sconces, but it was clear that no one was inside.

The two other comrades came back and shook their heads saying nothing was found. Holds made the gesture for them to go in. Gene was not looking forward to this at all.

They entered the room and they started to take in the feel and look of the place.

Holds broke the silence with a lowered voice, but still audible, "You two take the stairs up and see what you can find. Newly, we'll go down." Gene walked over to the stairwell, letting the other two ahead to climb up the stairs. He and Holds descended.

This place was a little eerie. The closer they got to the bottom, the darker it became. They should have grabbed one of the torches. A light shone up ahead, illuminating some of the steps. Once they reached the bottom, the light was from another small scone. The place was dark, cold, and musty.

There was nothing but a single door and another man slumped to the ground. Holds determined yet again that the man was dead. He started rifling through his pockets. Gene was about to ask what he was doing but Holds suddenly came away from the dead man with a key.

Of course, the man was guarding the door. This place did kind of remind Gene of the dungeons underneath his stronghold.

Holds placed the key in the lock and went to turn it.

"Wait," Gene said and placed a hand over Holds stopping his progress. "We don't know who they have in there. What if he's a killer?"

"We won't know unless we open it," Holds hissed back. "It's not like this door has a window we can look in." Gene was still unsure. Holds pulled his short knife out of its sheath with his free hand. "I got protection and usually prisoners don't have weapons." He made a fair point.

Gene sighed in resignation and took back his hand, letting Holds finish the job of opening the cell door. The lock disengaged and Holds squeezed the handle and pulled it open just a small amount. Gene was on the other side of the door, where he was blocked from the view of the inside of the cell. He had his hunting knife ready.

"You are not going to believe this Newly," he said under his breath. As Holds opened the door wide enough for Gene to look through, he was startled. Who they found, was not what they were expecting.

Chapter 2
Free at Last

She didn't know if what she did was right or wrong. She just knew it had to be done. All she had year after year was the hope that was given to her in her visions. Just moments before, a vision came to her of some men, blue and green auras, full of life, taking her out of the tower, but it also showed them being killed by the guards if they tried to take her out.

It was a confusing vision, one that showed two different outcomes. She felt the vision's urgency for her to decide. That decision gave her clear instructions, and she followed through.

And now, standing in the open doorway of the cell stood two men, one with a green aura and the other with a bluish-green aura. They didn't come in immediately. Their heads poked in, and their eyes moved about the room.

They were cautious. The bluish-green aura man stepped forward slowly with the green aura man moving the opposite direction. Both men's eyes darted around the room, maybe trying to see anything amongst the shadows. Nothing was there, she would know.

The bluish-green man finally came out of his stealthy walk and with a nod decided that there was nothing else in here. She saw him swiftly put something away that he had in his hand. He came over to her and knelt in front of her.

She wasn't scared, just apprehensive. This was the closest someone has been to her without hurting her since she can remember.

"Hello there," he said. His voice wasn't harsh, it had a soothing quality to it. "Are you alone down here?"

He was talking to her. She stopped talking just shortly after she was brought here. No one said anything to her before, all they did was give her food and drink and left her in here. They didn't even say anything when they came to torture her.

"Do you know why you are here?" She asked that question herself and never got an answer. The man's nose twitched, and his brow scrunched but he stayed where he was, asking with his eyes. His eyes closely matched the color of his aura. They were more green than blue, but what was behind those eyes was what made these men different from the others she'd been surrounded by these past years.

"Come on Holds, it smells horrible in here," the other man said. He held the back of his hand against his nose. She didn't blame him. It probably did smell in here. She just got so used to it that she didn't recognize it anymore.

The man named Holds gave a stern look at the other man. "How did you ever become a mayor? You are such a weakling."

"Same as you, I inherited the post from my father." Holds rolled his eyes at the man's response. He turned his attention back to her.

"We aren't here to harm you. My name is Penn and that's Newly," he pointed to the man. "What is your name?" She lowered her head looking at the floor. She didn't remember. There were a lot of things in the past she didn't want to remember so she closed them up with a wall in her mind. All the bad things were behind there, but there were a few other things too, like her name. She wasn't willing to break that wall down to just try and remember her name.

"Clearly she hasn't spoken a word," Newly observed. "She might be in shock. Look at her, she is skin and bone. Let's just take her and go. I'm sure she'll talk eventually when she is scrubbed up, clothed, and fed." Penn stood looking down at her, assessing.

"We can't take her with us *and* finish the mission."

"Are you saying to just leave her here? There is no one here Holds."

"What do you suggest?" Two other men came down the stairs with blue auras and stood in the doorway taking in the scene.

Newly continued, "Those two didn't find anyone and it wasn't like they were treating her the way a child is supposed to be treated anyways. Good riddance to them. They deserved what they got."

"If they weren't already dead, I would have done it after finding her."

"I suggest that one of us can take the girl back to your stronghold and the other three can continue on with the mission."

"Are you volunteering yourself to take the girl Newly?"

"Me? Well, I guess I am," he straightened up and gave a confident nod. Penn chuckled, obviously finding the situation funny.

"Fine. You might have had the idea for the mission, but you truly are not cut out for camping and fighting. You must have grown up in a bubble," He slapped the man on the back. Penn moved toward the other two and then Newly was kneeling in front of her.

He brought his hand up to his nose again. "Sorry about that, Holds can be a bit mean, but he means well. I'm Gene by the way. Let's get you out of here, okay?" He rose and made his way toward the door. The other men had already started to move back up the staircase. She stood there rooted to the same spot as when they entered. "Come on," he waved at her to head over. They were not forcing her. They were letting her make the decision.

She decided to trust them and took her first steps toward the door. That Spark inside her grew a tiny bit brighter. She had waited so long to leave this place and now it was finally happening. She followed Gene up the staircase. When they reached the top and moved outside of the tower, she took a deep breath.

It was heaven. The cool air rushed into her lungs, clear and untainted, opposite the air in her dungeon. She looked around her, seeing the surrounding trees. It was dark, but it wasn't as dark as she was used to. She looked up and around the tree's tops and saw the twinkling lights of the sky.

She brought her gaze down and noticed her guide was striding toward some overgrowth. She hurried over. Her breathing was labored since she hadn't done any kind of running in a long time. She reached Gene and stood next to him as he surveyed the area. A light breeze ruffled against the leaves and bushes. It touched her skin and sent goosebumps along the surface. She shivered at the feeling.

Gene looked back at her and frowned. "Are you cold?" She thought it was obvious since she was wearing no shoes and what once was a dress that only went to her knees, holes were everywhere in the material and didn't protect her at all.

He bent down, removing the pack that was on his back. He dug in there until he pulled out a piece of clothing. He opened it up and came over and draped it around her shoulders. There were arm holes, so she stuck her little limbs inside. He bent down and buttoned up the front of the clothing.

"There you go. It's all I got but hopefully it will keep you warm." He looked down at her feet and frowned again. He went back to his pack and dug around inside. A minute later he produced two cloth looking tubes. He held the material out to her. "Put these on your feet. I don't have any extra shoes so these socks will have to do. I cannot let you walk around barefoot."

She took the offered clothing and gingerly sat down. She tugged each foot in and then stood up. Everything was big, but he was right, it was keeping her warm.

"Holds and the others are heading south a little way, hoping to set up camp for the night away from here. I don't think we should stay around this place either. We'll head back west for a little bit and then we will rest. Stay close to me." He placed his pack back on and headed in the direction he indicated.

This was it, her first steps toward freedom. She wasn't going back in that tower again, so the only option was to follow Gene and hope that everything would be better from now on. Anything was better than being in that dark hole. She was brought out of the darkness and now she would let light fill her back up.

Chapter 3
Marvel Inn

A few days later they reached Holds Stronghold. The journey wasn't too long since they left their horses in the care of a farmer that lived at the base of the mountains just west of Obern Forest. Gene collected his horse and road the rest of the way with the little girl.

He felt bad about his continued reaction to the small child's condition. Thankfully they passed a stream and they washed some of the grime that was stuck to her. She still hadn't spoken, but she seemed to understand that Gene was there to help her.

In the past three years, Brosch had demanded that strongholds be searched for children with the Might. Any child that was found with it was taken. If the stronghold refused, then the tyrant just seized the stronghold and then would just kill the children instead of taking them. People got smart and realized it was better for their child to be taken, knowing that they were alive, then them ending up dead because the adults were unwilling to follow orders.

It was barbaric and frightening, countless innocent children died at his hand. Now, children would be taken from families and were never heard from again. It was an injustice. He needed to be stopped.

But people were too afraid to stand against him. Gene knew that he had to do something, even though he was new to his post as mayor, it didn't matter. He had his beliefs, and he knew that someday the information they gather from this expedition will help.

He reached the main throughway into Holds Stronghold. It was one of the most defensive locations for a stronghold in all Hockland. There was the sea on the west side, mountains to the north, and a swift flowing river to the east cutting southwest that dumped into the sea and can only be crossed by the one bridge that led to the stronghold.

The girl always seemed to be awake and alert. It was strange, he was unsure if she slept during their two-day journey. As they came close to the stronghold she sat forward in the saddle, taking in the buildings outside and inside the stronghold.

Mostly farmers of crops and livestock occupied the area outside the walls. Their little homes dotted throughout the area. The closer they came to the walls, the thicker the houses and shops became. They passed through the open gates where sentinels stood watch. He was sure that they would make sure that unsavory folk were scrutinized closer.

Gene guided his horse along the cobblestone streets. He was headed toward the Marvel Inn, where he had been staying before leaving on the mission. Well, now his mission had changed. He was to make sure this girl had a good place to stay and build her strength so they can possibly get information about Brosch's Stronghold from her.

They reached the inn and he dismounted. He held up his hands for her to take. She dangled her legs to the side and hopped off. She was a small thing, but the first time he tried to lift her off, she silently refused to let him, so all he could do was offer to help her.

He strode to the door, knowing that she would follow behind. A stable hand sat there. He flipped a coin at the young boy. "Be a good lad and take good care of my horse."

"Will do sir," the boy said after clutching the coin in his hand. He scurried over to the horse and led the animal to the stables attached to the inn.

Gene pulled open the door and stepped inside. He was greeted with a blast of warm air. The main room had tables about it, some patrons sat eating supper, some enjoying a drink, or playing dice. He strode through to the innkeeper that he had met prior to leaving. The large man with an apron around his gut looked up from wiping down the bar.

"Ah, sir, welcome back," the innkeeper gave him a friendly smile.

"Thank you. I would like to acquire a second room."

"A second one?" The innkeeper raised his brow in question.

"Yes. I have a traveler with me that will need her own room and request that a bath be brought up and food prepared." The innkeeper peeked around him and then his eyes shot down to the little girl that was standing just behind him. She looked at the innkeeper hesitantly with those large hazel eyes. She looked so small in his clothes.

Gene noticed the innkeeper softened right up with one look at her. "Of course, we'll set the little miss up."

"Great, also, she will need some clothes as well. Everything that she would need, a few dresses, undergarments, shoes, nightgown, whatever." He reached into his pouch and produced five coins and placed them on the bar.

The innkeeper reached for the coins and drew them closer to him. "I will make the arrangements. Gertie! Get room three prepared for a bath!" he yelled to the doorway behind him. The large man turned back toward Gene. "The room next to yours is open and that is where the little miss can stay. While it is getting ready, take a seat and I'll bring out some food. Looks like she needs it."

"Thank you." Gene started walking toward an empty table in the middle of the room. He felt the eyes of the other patrons glance over at them since he was certain the girl was following him. He sat facing the wall so he could survey the room. The little girl stopped next to him.

He smiled softly at her and gestured toward the chair opposite him. "Have a seat little one. The man at the bar will bring us out something warm to eat." The girl nodded and sat in the seat across from him. She looked like a doll that got left outside too long. Her dark hair was matted, and it hung around her in strings, sometimes hanging in the front of her pale face. Her eyes were sunken in, and she really did look like she would collapse at any moment.

Before he could try talking with her again like he did every night, food arrived on the arms of the innkeeper. He placed a large helping in front of Gene with ale and an equally large helping in front of the girl. He placed a glass down in front of her. Gene raised an eyebrow at him.

"It's just milk. I don't give kids ale." He harrumphed and went back toward the bar. Gene took a large sip of ale and continued, breaking up the bread on his plate and dipping it into the stew in front of him.

She watched him as she always did. He noticed that she mimicked him in a way. She took a sip of her drink and then proceeded to break small chunks of bread and dipping it in the stew like he was doing. He saw her eyes get large at the first bit. She started to eat a slight bit faster taking in large portions of food.

"Slow down there little one. You don't want to get sick by putting too much food in your belly." He chuckled at her look and the slower movements she made. It had been an interesting two-day journeying with this girl. She must have been through so much, but he was still unsuccessful with his questioning. So instead, he just didn't ask questions anymore.

"I got you a room and they are putting a bath up there for you. After you're down eating, I'll make sure you have some help with the bath. They're going to find you some proper fitting clothes as well. We'll just throw away what you have on. That includes my stuff too." He felt a little bad, but her stink penetrated his clothes, and he knew there was no amount of cleaning that was going to clear that smell out of the fibers.

He continued with a mouthful of food, "We can spend a couple days here for you to eat and rest and then I can take you about the city. I must wait a bit until Holds returns to see what we are going to do with you. Since you haven't told us anything about yourself, we don't know where you belong." She sat there like always, quietly eating. Gene just had to be patient, eventually she would talk.

A short time later, Gertie came over and announced the bath was ready. Gene insisted that the girl would need help and Gertie was kind enough to offer to do that. The girl was led away. She did look back a few times to make sure he was still there, which he was. He understood that he was that little girl's lifeline. If it wasn't for their group being slightly off course, they would have never come upon the tower.

Gene continued to sip some ale and started to think. There was a reason that girl was in the tower. He wondered being so close to Brosch Stronghold if it was one of the children he had taken that had the Might. He didn't know how that worked, figuring out who had it or not. Since he didn't have the Might, he did not have the ability to find others with the Might. Only people with ability can find others with ability.

He was getting tired from the long travel. His musings can wait another day. He took the stairs and continued to his room was. He passed room three on his way. As he turned the lock to enter his room, Gertie exited from room three. She shut the door and looked over at him.

"She's all settled for the night. She's not one for talking, is she?"

"No, she's not. Can you have a bath brought up to me in the morning?"

"Will do sir," Gertie nodded and headed back toward the stairs. He didn't know what was going to happen to the little girl, but at least he knew that he was helping her now, and that he would risk everything to help other children like her.

Chapter 4
Fate's Path

She's been at Holds Stronghold four days now. As she sat in front of the mirror, she did her hair up like Gertie did the other day. She brushed her long raven locks, twisted and braided here and there, ending with her hair pulled back away from her face but her long hair was still free down her back. She was a whole different person than when she arrived.

Gene had treated her with kindness, making sure she had everything she needed. She was wearing a green dress and brown shoes. Her feet felt funny since she couldn't remember the last time she wore any shoes. These came up and covered her ankle. The dress was loose on her frame, but Gertie said it should fit fine once she had some good meals in her.

At first, she thought she was a different kind of prisoner, but she quickly shoved that thought aside. Gene never forced her to do anything. He told her what was going to happen and then he waited for her to decide. Also, she got a warm bed to sleep in if she wished, warm clothes, and as much food as she could eat. This was not at all like the tower.

A sharp knock sounded on the door before it was pushed in. Gene's face peaked around. "You're up I see." He let himself in. He also was very different looking than when they first met. His green aura matched perfectly with his eyes, and they seemed to stand out against his dark hair. He was clean shaven and had on cleaned and pressed clothing. It was nothing like his rugged travel wear.

"Holds arrived back during the night. We need to go and talk with him to find out what is the best course of action to take regarding your protection." She nodded in understanding. Children belonged with someone. She noticed in the last few days walking around the city with Gene that the little ones were always with an adult or were close by adults. They were watched and kept safe, just like Gene had done for her as they were walking. The problem was, she didn't know where she belonged.

"Let's get that cloak on, it's a tad chilly outside this morning. That is one thing I don't have to worry about back home. It stays a perfect temperature all year round." She swung the cloak around her shoulders and clasped the front.

He stood by the door and had opened it wide for her to exit first. She walked out by him and down the steps. He was close behind her as they made their way through the inn and out the door to the street beyond. He led her from there toward the north end of the city.

She was still a little out of breath once they made it to a large structure. She knew she didn't have a lot of strength, but she felt like she was getting better every day. They approached the main doors where two men stood to each side.

Upon seeing them come near, one man turned and opened the door for them. Gene nodded and continued through. It was nice that she felt like a regular person now. Unlike the few stops they made on their way here from the tower, people constantly wondered what was wrong with her and why she looked the way she did. She didn't hear any of that in Holds Stronghold, which was a relief.

Gene walked to the right of the front entrance and knocked on a closed door. The door was opened, and they walked in. She didn't know what kind of room this was, but it was roomy, with a fireplace that had chairs around it and a desk in the corner, where Penn sat. Penn looked up from a piece of paper that he was holding.

"Newly," he addressed Gene and turned his gaze to her. His expression turned to awe. "Is this the same girl from the tower?" He slowly stood and came around the desk.

"It is Holds."

He knelt in front of her and assessed her appearance. He scrunched his brow but then smiled at her. "She looks much better. Still a little thin but better." He stood and made his way back to his seat.

"We have to discuss where she will go."

"Has she spoken?"

"She has not," Gene shook his head from side to side. "What if she truly can't speak? I know she can hear and obviously see, but speaking, that hasn't happened."

"I guess we will have to assign her a caregiver. I'm tempted to sign you up for the job," Penn smirked.

"Oh no. Not that I didn't enjoy spending time with her, I am not prepared to raise any children."

"What? Not prepared?"

"I have many responsibilities as the new mayor of my stronghold, and I just wouldn't be able to spend the time needed to make sure she is nurtured. Plus, I have no idea how to take care of children"

"It's not like she's a wee one still learning how to crawl and walk around."

"I know, but I'll be traveling a lot and it just wouldn't be right for her to just stay at the stronghold. I don't have a wife. All those woman things that come up, I would not be comfortable handling that."

"I like it when you are uncomfortable. It makes me laugh," Penn smiled with obvious mirth.

"Why don't you take her Holds?" Penn's smile faded quickly at that suggestion.

"No."

"And the reason?" Gene prodded.

"Same as yours I guess."

"Alright, then who do you know that would take on a young girl and be someone that we would trust with the knowledge of how she was found?" Both men thought for a few seconds. She looked between the two seeing little shoots of color flare from their aura. They were small, like tiny flames. It was a beauty to see.

Holds suggested, "What about Jebrow?"

"Kalvin Jebrow?"

"The very one. His stronghold is in the south, far from Brosch and I do remember that he has some children around the girl's age." She could see Gene contemplating it.

"I think that is an exceptional choice."

"Perfect, I'll send him a letter informing him of the situation. Of course, details will not be added, but he should be able to get the drift."

"When will we leave?"

"I have no idea if Brosch is looking for this girl, and if he is, there is a possibility his cronies are looking. It's probably best that we travel at night."

"Are you coming with us then?"

"I suppose so. I have business to discuss with Jebrow anyway. We can take the throughway that leads through Jergon Forest and pops out just south of your stronghold. Then it's a straight shot south to Jebrow."

"When do we leave?" Gene asked.

"Might as well leave tonight. The sooner we leave the area with her the better."

Gene led her back out of the room and out of what seemed to be Holds home. They headed back to the inn. "I hope you're ready for an adventure little one." She hoped so too.

When evening fell, she gathered up her new items and was placing them in her own saddlebag. Gene wanted to make sure she had her own horse to ride. They met up with Holds and a few of his men would accompany them. Once everyone was set for the weeklong journey, they headed out. Although it was night, the moon was full that night, shining down on them.

As she looked up into the sky full of twinkling stars, she realized she had seen this before. It was the vision that had kept a small kernel of hope inside her at the start of her confinement in the tower. Here she was, traveling among the moon and stars with men who would protect her and take her far away from the tower. Knowing that vision had come to pass made her Spark pulse.

She was going home.

Chapter 5
The Jebrows

Penn was thankful that the long trip was finally coming to an end. Newly parted ways two days ago, deciding he needed to take care of some business matters at his stronghold. Penn didn't blame him. It was hard to be away from home and try to keep everything running smoothly.

Just as Newly felt that it was his responsibility to make sure the girl was cared for, so did Penn. Jebrow was the only one that he knew of that his children did not get taken away or killed. His stronghold had been attacked by Brosch and it has been slow to rebuild the surrounding farm and livestock community. The Capton Stronghold just to the west took the most damage out of all the strongholds during the Great War. That stronghold was currently unoccupied and there were few that stayed in the surrounding area at the start, but now it was a no-man's land. The whole Capton family was murdered by Brosch's cronies.

It was sad to think that such innocent lives were taken. He'd think they spared the children, but they didn't, confirming that they all had the Might since both Mayor Capton and his lady had ability. It was depressing news, and it was a warning to other strongholds that didn't answer to Brosch's wishes what would happen to theirs if they didn't comply.

Penn had to get his mind in the right focus. His idea and Newly's aligned. They had to do something to save the innocent children that were being taken. The girl that rode next to him was testament of their commitment to their cause. Even to them, saving one child, was worth it.

They came across the outskirts of Jebrow Stronghold. Since his last visit two years ago, the surrounding villages have started to look good. There were still a few settlements that showed damage by fire, but they were starting to be few and far between. The walls of the stronghold took severe damage and there were still areas of derelict, but Penn noticed that they were concentrating their efforts on the rebuilding of the wall as he saw a group of men working on one of the areas.

Penn's small entourage made their way through the gates. Most of the city folk didn't pay attention to the group's movements. They made their way directly to Jebrow's home. Penn hoped that Jebrow had received his correspondence and would be expecting them.

He stopped directly in front of the home and dismounted. He came over to the girl to help her, but before he could she had slid off the horse herself. She was very independent which was good. Plus, she did not like to be touched, even as simple as a pat on the shoulder she noticeable twitched.

Penn made his way up the steps where one guard was standing beside the door. He approached with the girl at his side, his other men stayed with the horses. The guard nodded and opened the door for them. He was apparently expected.

They made their way straight ahead through the entrance to a set of doors that were already opened. As he and the girl made their way into Jebrow's study, the man himself was sitting behind his desk. He looked up as they approached.

"Ah, Holds my good man. I wondered when you'd be arriving." The man rose from his seat and came around his desk to shake Penn's hand.

"It took us an extra day since we had a special traveler with us."

"Yes, in the note you said something about a girl," Jebrow turned to the child in question. "And this is she?" The girl was looking at Jebrow with wide eyes. She didn't look afraid, just in deep concentration, like she was trying to figure out a puzzle. "And what is your name?" Jebrow asked her.

"She doesn't speak. Well, she hasn't spoken since we rescued her."

"Interesting. It's been a long trip for you, hasn't it?" He addressed the girl. "I think a good meal would lift your spirits. Maria!" he called out the door.

A small woman in a plain house dress came into the room. "Yes sir?"

"Why don't you take this charming young lady to the kitchen and get her something to eat? I'll be along shortly."

"Of course," she curtsied and came over to the girl. She went to grab her hand, but the girl evaded her and stepped away.

"She doesn't like to be touched, Jebrow. Just have the woman lead the way and she'll follow."

"You hear that, Maria? No touching." Jebrow turned to the girl. "Go on with Maria. She won't harm you. She'll lead you to the kitchen." The girl looked between the three of them and settled her gaze on Penn. Penn nodded toward the door indicating that she should go with Maria. The girl bowed her head and started following Maria.

"I take it she wasn't found in the best of conditions," Jebrow said as he went back around his desk and took a seat in his chair. He indicated to Penn to also have a seat.

Penn began the lengthy story of how they came upon the tower and how they found the girl in the dungeon. As he was relaying the story, Jebrow's expression turned menacing, and his blue eyes flashed with vengeance.

"The only thing that we couldn't figure out was what happened to the guards at the tower. When we arrived, every single one of them were dead."

"From what?"

"That's just it. There was no sign of any physical damage. Although, each one had a look of intense pain on their faces, so they looked to have been tortured to death. We figured it could have been something they ate."

"The girl was unaffected?"

"She was the only living soul we found at that tower. She was close to death herself." Penn glanced at the door thinking about how she looked when they first found her. "She looked like a walking skeleton Jebrow. How could any man let that happen to a child?"

"Indeed. Well, at least the guards got what they deserved. However, I'm inclined to think they were acting under Brosch's orders. The question is, who is she? She would be the only one who would know that answer, and yet, she doesn't speak."

"I believe she can and chooses not to. Maybe she'll come around."

"Maybe. Children can be resilient. Let's hope that she didn't give up on life when she was in that tower. If she harbored hope, then she'll come around."

"I have other business to discuss with you as well."

"Yes. Before we start that discussion, let's go make sure the girl is introduced to my family. You will stay for supper of course and we can talk business afterward."

"Sounds good." Jebrow rose and made his way out the study and headed to the kitchen. Penn followed. He was interested in seeing the girl's reactions to Jebrow's children, if she even reacted at all.

Chapter 6
Missing Aura

She didn't eat much of what Maria had gathered for her. She was too nervous to eat. Mr. Jebrow had a wonderful glowing blue aura. It was so bright, and he was so full of light. She was curious as to how one person can hold so much life inside, so much promise. It was a puzzle to be sure.

It didn't take him long to appear in the kitchen, with Penn in tow.

"There she is. I hope you had enough to eat?" She looked up into his eyes, blue as the sky. He wasn't as intimidating when her mind was thinking of fluffy clouds. "Come. I want you to meet the rest of the family." He gestured for her to follow him out the door.

She decided there wasn't any harm in meeting this family. He moved gracefully through the house and made his way to a glass door that slid open. He stepped out into a large grassy area, where there was a small pond. Beyond the pond was a wall. She assumed that was the wall of the stronghold that wrapped around the whole city.

Mr. Jebrow continued toward a group of people that were sitting on the lawn close to the pond. Two women sat in chairs and there were three others running around. They were small, like her, so she assumed that they could be children. As they approached, Mr. Jebrow clapped his hands twice and called out.

"Alright children, stop with what you are doing. I would like to introduce you to someone." He made his way to a beautiful yellow-aura lady. Her golden hair seemed to make a halo above her head. Mr. Jebrow kissed her on the cheek affectionately and then stood in front of the children.

There were three of them, two girls and a boy. Mr. Jebrow motioned behind him for her to approach. She did so, stopping just beside him. Penn was close by but stayed his distance. He wouldn't let anything bad happen to her.

"Children, I would like you to meet," he paused, looking down at her remembering in that moment that he did not know her name. He squinted his eyes and then blurted out a name. "Eva. This is Eva and she will be staying with us."

Eva. That sounded like a nice name. She will think on if she will keep it or not. He moved her by directing a hand just behind her, like he was steering her without touching her. They were standing in front of the two girls.

"Eva, meet my two daughters, Sasha and Sonya." The two girl's auras were identical. They were yellow orange, much like the center of the sun. Like Mr. Jebrow and the yellow-aura woman, their auras seemed extra bright. It was hard to continue to look at them.

"And this," Mr. Jebrow maneuvered her to stand in front of the boy, "is my son, Jace." She tentatively looked up, thinking that she would get the same glaring aura. However, when she looked at this boy, there was no aura. Odd. Everyone had an aura that she knew of. Even the older plumb lady sitting on the other chair had an aura, although not as bright as these family members.

She didn't know what to say. She just stared in fascination. She took in every detail, from his blue-green eyes and his brown hair that had some streaks of golden blonde. He was wearing nice fitting clothes. He was just slightly taller than she and he stood with an assessing eye. He was a mystery for sure, and she hoped to figure all that out.

"Now, I must attend to some business. Make Eva feel welcomed. She will be staying with us for a while," Mr. Jebrow addressed his children. He turned to Eva, even though she really wasn't paying attention. All her focus was on the boy named Jace. "If you need anything Eva, you can ask my wife Lady Jebrow or the governess Ms. Kelfer. I will see you all at supper." He turned and headed back to the house with Penn in tow.

What was she to do now? It seemed like Jace was also staring at her. He raised an eyebrow and had a small smirk on his face.

"Alright children, back to your lessons. Eva, you can join Sasha and Sonya over here," Ms. Kelfer indicated to a spot near her where there were some black boards and some white sticks. Jace winked at her and turned and walked toward the pond. What was that for?

She slowly made her way over to the governess, even as she watched Jace retreat to another location. She slowly sat down next to one of the girls. She wasn't sure what they were doing, but she was a quick learner. She was sure she would be able to pick it up.

"Eva, here you go," Sonya, or was it Sasha, handed her a black board and a white stick. She looked over at the girls and saw that they had the boards on their lap and the white stick in their hand. She did the same.

"Now, I would like you to write the word, 'population.'" The girls bent forward and started to make shapes on the board. She mimicked them. However, she could tell that her markings were a little sloppy compared to theirs. "Very good," Ms. Kelfer continued. "The next word I would like you to write is 'stronghold.'"

This continued for a while. She sat and drew on the board, not sure exactly what she was doing, but the scribbles started to get better and were not as sloppy. Once the lesson was over, Ms. Kelfer said they could go and play. The two girls immediately rose and ran off with a squeal.

Eva wasn't sure exactly what to do. She went in the direction of the girls, who seemed to be heading toward a grouping of trees where a board attached to some rope swung from a branch. She stopped about halfway there, and her gaze went in the direction of the pond.

There Jace sat, leaned up against a lone tree. He had something in his hands and his eyes looked to be scanning over the item. As if her feet had a mind of their own, she made her way down to the pond.

She stopped right in front of Jace, mere inches away from where his feet stretched out in front of him. She was looking at the top of his head, since it was slightly bowed as his eyes scanned the item in his hands. She at first thought that he didn't notice her, but then he spoke.

"Is there something I can help you with?" he asked without looking up at her. She continued to stare at him, not sure what to do. Her hands twisted in front of her. She wanted to be sure that he had a Spark. She was unable to detect an aura, but he had to have a Spark. She never saw a Spark without an aura.

He sighed and closed the item in his hand and looked up at her. Those eyes pierced right into her. Her breath caught at the color. They were so clear and vibrant. Not as light as his father's eyes, darker, like he had something brewing below the surface.

"Go run along. I'm sure my sisters can keep you entertained." She felt a tug at her conscious that she should do as he asked. He knew what was best. But that wasn't right. She blinked a few times to clear that feeling away. She wasn't interested in what his sisters were doing. She was interested in what he was doing.

His brow scrunched up as he was unsure why she still stood there. She was asking herself the same question. "I guess it doesn't matter what you do. I'll just ignore you." He bent his head back down to the item he had and opened it back up. She wanted to know what it was, so she made her way over beside him and sat down.

Chapter 7
Strange Connection

Great, now she was sitting next to him. The new girl, Eva, was looking at his book over his shoulder. It was bad enough that she just stared at him, but now she was staring at what he was doing. He didn't know that someone could be more annoying than his sisters. Although Jace found her annoying, he was also interested in finding out who this mysterious girl was.

As declared by his father, the girl's name was Eva. She was a small wisp of a thing. She was just slightly taller than his sisters but almost sickly thin. It made her hazel eyes even larger, and her skin was translucent making her black hair seem intensely dark. But he could tell her eyes were searching and taking in everything around her.

Like right now, her brow was scrunched as she was looking at his book. If she was staying for a while, which it sounded like it from the conversations he heard streaming from his father's study the last week, then she was probably going to continue to do just what she was doing right now.

He sighed in resignation and said without turning toward her, "It's a book about farming." She didn't comment. He decided to continue. "I'm currently reading about crop rotation and the importance of not planting the same things over and over again in the same spot." She still did not say anything.

Of course, he was curious and decided to turn and look at her sitting next to him. He saw her gaze was scanning over the pages, probably trying to locate where he was seeing this information.

"See," he pointed to the paragraph he was currently reading, "It says it right here that certain plants give nutrients to the soil and other plants take it out of the soil." She still had that slightly scrunched brow like she was figuring out a puzzle.

"You can read right?" he asked her. Her gaze slowly moved from the book and looked at him. Their eyes locked together and Jace felt a sort of tingle down his spine. Surprisingly it wasn't an uncomfortable feeling, just odd.

After a moment her gaze dropped down and she slowly shook her head side to side.

"Oh, I didn't know that. You seemed really interested so I thought you were reading over my shoulder." If she couldn't read, then what was she doing looking over his shoulder? With her gaze on the ground, she plucked at something invisible on her dress looking slightly embarrassed by the fact that she couldn't read.

He didn't want to make her feel like that. Not everyone in the village could read, so it wasn't rare to find someone that could not.

"Do you want to learn how?" Her gaze popped back up to his and they looked to be shimmering in waited anticipation. "I'll take that as a, yes?" She eagerly nodded her head. Jace couldn't help but smile at her. Her own mouth twitched slightly at the corners. One day he would get her to smile better than that.

"Well, we aren't going to learn with this, as fascinating as this subject is", he said sarcastically. "It's not good for a newbie." He closed the book and rose to his feet. He stretched his limbs out since he was sitting for quite a while before she came over.

"Come on. Let's go look for a book for you." He gestured for her to follow him and started toward the house. She quickly got to her feet and fell into step next to him. They made their way through the sliding door and continued past his father's study and the staircase. On the other side of the staircase was the library.

He knew that he was lucky being a mayor's son. He was born into wealth and privilege. He had the best of everything, and that included book options. He figured that it wasn't a big deal teaching Eva to read, it gave him something else to do besides continuing to read about how to run a stronghold. All he wanted to do was practice fighting and go fishing and climb trees. He hated just sitting around reading. If he was going to sit around, he wanted to be doing something productive.

Jace went to a specific section of the library where he scanned the lower shelves. These were easily accessible by children and his father often put books for them down at this level. He could see out of the corner of his eye that Eva was looking about the room with an expression of awe on her face. She probably wasn't used to seeing this many books. He had a niggling feeling at the base of his skull that she hadn't seen much of anything in her short life.

Shaking that thought out of his head, he selected a book on children's fairy tales. These were common throughout the country. He remembered when his Nanna would tell them to him just before nodding off to sleep.

"Here we go. We'll start with this one." He moved to the love seat and plopped down on the edge. He moved back, but his legs weren't long enough yet, so his feet were still a few inches from the ground.

He patted the seat next to him, saying Eva should join. She bounded over to the seat and scrambled up the front. She turned herself around and sat down very close to him. Not even an inch separated them. Jace opened the book on his lap and slid the book partially onto her lap.

"Okay, before we start, I do have a question for you." He waited until she looked over at him from her seat. Once their eyes locked, he asked his question. "Can you speak?"

He saw her lips form in a thin line, and she glanced away slightly before returning her gaze to his. "I ask because it is easier to read if you can do it out loud so I can hear what you are doing, in case there is something that needs to be fixed."

She was biting her bottom lip with her teeth, and he thought she wouldn't answer until she slowly moved her head up and down. He visibly sighed. Well, that was a relief.

"Great, let's get started." He turned to the book as a reference. "First, you need to know your alphabet so you can figure out the words you are reading, like this first word is 'once.' It has an o, n, c, and e. Each letter was a sound so when you put the sounds together, you get a word. Do you know your alphabet?" he asked waiting for her response.

She shook her head as a no. Still not wanting to talk. Well, at this point he knew she could since she admitted just a moment ago and it was just a matter of time until she did start talking.

"Well, there are twenty-six letters in the alphabet. There is a, b, c, d," he paused and saw that she had her brow scrunched again. Maybe it would be easier for her to see the letters. He thought for a second if it would be better to point them out in the book or if he should go get a writing board and chalk.

"You probably don't know what I am talking about unless you can see it, right?" Jace looked down at the book, and then at his hands, then at her hands. That's it! He could just trace the letters in her palm.

"I know what will help, here." He grabbed her hand to trace on her palm, but he got zapped. He immediately dropped her hand and shook his to try and shake away the pain. It wasn't much, but it still was unexpected.

"Don't know what happened there. You willing to try again?" He held his hand out, waiting for her to place her hand in his. She looked at his hand, like there could be something wrong with it. "It's nothing to worry about. People create energy all the time so it would make sense that some could have released or something." He tried to remember what his Nanna told him about auras and energy, but he didn't fully understand the concept and now that she was gone, he didn't have anyone else to ask.

Eva only took another few seconds and decided to place her hand, palm facing up in his open hand. As their skin touched, he felt a tiny vibration, but nothing like the shock when they first touched. It was odd, but not painful, so he decided to ignore it and he would figure out what was going on later.

"Okay, I'm going to trace the letters into your palm and also indicate the sound for each letter." He went through each letter tracing and saying the sounds associated. Every time his finger traced over her skin, there was this pulling sensation. Towards the end of the alphabet, he felt tired, like tracing was using a lot of his energy.

Once he completed, he let go of her hand and it felt like a weight was lifted. It was a weird feeling he was unable to understand. He swiped the back of his hand across his brow, realizing that it was wet from his sweat.

"Well, I think that's it for today. We'll continue tomorrow," he gave her a shrug and a lopsided smile. Eva gave him a look of concern as she pointed at his face.

"I'm okay, just tired," he closed the book and stood up to replace it back on the shelf. He turned back and saw her head bent and she was fidgeting with her hands. That was what she must do when she was nervous.

He came over to her and placed his hand over her fidgeting ones. There was that feeling again but he wanted to make sure she knew he was fine. He removed his hand, and he went back to normal but of course still tired. Her eyes slowly rose to his and he could see the uncertainty in them.

"Hey, you didn't do anything wrong. Eventually we must figure out what is going on between our hands, but for now, I'm going and taking a nap before supper." He walked toward the door to go regain his energy through sleep.

Jace stopped and turned toward her, where she still sat on the love seat, looking at him with those large eyes. He didn't know what it was about her, he just felt like she needed him. He smiled at her and gave her a wink and went on his way.

Chapter 8
Nighttime Visit

A week had passed since the incident between Eva and Jace. As she sat in the room the family gave her, she held open the book that she and Jace had been working out of. They both had avoided touching hands during their time together. That was good for her because she was trying to understand what had been transferred.

She knew she gained something through physical contact with Jace. She felt this orb inside her start to glow. It was like whatever she was getting from Jace enlivened her. But what was the cost?

She thought back on how Jace become very tired, and he said something about energy. Was that connected with auras? Was she taking his energy? It seemed that would be a possibility, but she wasn't willing to try and touch another person to find out.

Well, as soon as she learned how to read, then she could just find the answer she needed in one of the many books in Mr. Jebrow's library. She bent over the book and dragged her index finger across the lines filled with different words.

As the day become night, darkness descended around her. She'd lived in the dark for so long it was like an old friend greeting her. There was a significant difference though being here at Jebrow Stronghold. She closed the book and set it on the bed, she rose to her feet and her soft footfalls took her to the huge floor to ceiling windows. She looked out and up and saw all those little twinkling lights and the moon which was waning.

She would have never seen this gorgeous view if she was left in the tower dungeon. This darkness showed the life and light within it. She didn't have to second guess what lurked in the shadows, because this place didn't have those types of shadows.

The Jebrow family was growing on her. Their bright auras and continued support with her transition made her Spark glow a little brighter each day.

She still had a long way to go trusting the Jebrow's. The times when she was with Jace, she occasionally felt an urge to trust him. She always second guessed it though because she was experiencing something she couldn't explain. This was why learning to read was so crucial.

The family didn't know this about her, but Eva did not sleep. Unlike everyone else that needs to close their eyes and spend time in the land of dreams to regain energy, she did not. Ever since being in the tower, she had not done this activity. She could not remember before that time since that carefully erected wall in her conscious was placed there for a reason.

The reason was because what lay beyond the wall was bad and those bad memories she didn't want to remember. Her life in the tower was bad enough and if she closed off other information, those memories must be worse.

The family must be asleep by now, but she wanted to show Jace what she had accomplished with reading today. She didn't want to wait until morning.

She crossed the room back to the bed and lifted the book up into her arms. She held the book to her chest like a precious jewel. She made her way out of her room and down the hall. She was given a tour of the home and she tended to wander around at night anyway. She was learning quite a bit about where everything was in this home, all those hidden servant stairs, and little hidey holes.

Eva slowed to a stop at a particular door. This room was Jace's. She took a deep calming breath and pushed the door open. It squeaked slightly as it swung wide. She peeked in and quickly scanned the interior. It was set-up much like her room with towering windows and a bed on the opposite side of the room. His though was twice as big and he had more stuff in his room. There were many toys and other items that seemed to be well used strewn about the place.

She made her way to the side of the bed and there he was. She could hear Jace's soft breathing, knowing that he was probably deep in sleep. She used a stool that was tucked slightly under the bed and climbed her way up.

There she sat looking down at him with the book in her lap. She nudged him on the shoulder. His breathing changed slightly but he didn't wake up. She nudged him again a little bit harder. His brow scrunched and he moved slightly. She gave him another nudge just to make sure he would wake.

His eyes slowly opened and then when they focused and landed on her he shot up in bed and tried to move as far away as possible. Her eyes widened and she was unsure what she had done.

Jace squinted at her and asked, "Eva?" He turned to his bedside table and lit a candle. The soft glow of light filled the space around them. He looked back over and sighed, "Eva, you scared me half to death!" He pinched the bridge of his nose.

She started to turn away. Maybe it was a bad idea to do this now. His hand shot toward her and landed on the sleeve of her nightgown, stopping her. "Don't go. Since you've already woke me, what do you want?" He looked at her with that crooked smile of his.

She made her way to the side of the bed that had the most room and settled herself on top of the sheets next to him. His eyebrow quirked as he watched her move about. Once she was propped up against the headrest, she opened the book in her lap.

She went to the first page and placed her finger on the first word. She closed her eyes a moment to find some inner strength. She hoped that he wouldn't make fun of her. She began to read aloud.

Chapter 9
The Sweetest Sound

The sound was mesmerizing. He blinked a few times and rubbed his eyes to make sure he wasn't dreaming. He even went so far as to pinch himself just to make sure. Jace's whole face lit up and he was smiling. Of course, Eva couldn't see that because she was bent over the book, slowly sounding out the words.

Her voice was so soft and musical. He wasn't really paying attention to what she was saying, just the fact that she was speaking. To him of all people! He felt honored at the chance to be the first to hear her sweet voice.

"Jace?" he blinked a few times realizing that she was now looking at him with a questioning look.

"Yeah?"

"Is this story true?" she asked just barely above a whisper. He could tell that she still wasn't quite sure about this talking business, so he needed to figure out a way that would make her more comfortable.

"Which story?" He bent forward to look at the pages she was looking at.

"Was there a warrior that was like this one in the story? It says he was strong and mighty. His ability helped heal the land and restore life to what was once dead. How can something dead be brought back to life? Once it's dead, that's it. You can't make it alive again."

He was right. She'll become a regular chatter box if she keeps up this pace. "These are children's stories, and some are based on truth. That doesn't mean that everything in the story is true. Some of it is made up to make the story seem more magical. Also, I think when this story talks about the land, it has plants and animals, and it is possible to grow things anew when a land looks like nothing is living. I think that is what they are referencing. It's not actually talking about bringing something back from the dead," he shuddered at that thought.

He agreed with her that death was final. He went hunting enough to know once the animal's Spark blinked out, that was it.

She slowly nodded her head, and he could tell that she understood what he was talking about since her brow wasn't scrunched up, but it was more reflective.

"Thanks for trusting me, Eva." He smiled over at her and looked into her hazel eyes that looked brown in the low lighting. The small smile that graced her face was worth the wait.

"Thanks for teaching me."

He waved his hand in the air. "It was nothing. You are obviously a good student and quick learner. Keep practicing and you'll get better."

"Can you teach me something else?" she asked, her head slightly tilted waiting.

"Like what?"

"Well," she started fidgeting with her fingers, her nervous habit.

"Eva, anything you say cannot make me think any different of you." She sat there for a bit, probably gathering up the courage to ask.

"I want to learn how to fight," she barely spoke loud enough for Jace to hear.

"Why would you want to learn how to fight?"

"So, I don't get taken again." He didn't know much about where Eva was before she came here to his family's home. But hearing about someone taking her got his blood boiling.

"Why would anyone take you? I would not allow it to happen." He spoke the truth. It was hard to believe, but he felt this need to be her protector. He would fight for her.

"What if you are gone or I am alone? I don't want to be helpless."

"That's asking a lot of me." Her head drooped and shoulders slumped, already taking his answer as a no.

He chanced it. He reached over and put his fingers under her chin to tilt her head back up. That weird feeling came, but it wasn't like he feared it, only scared about not knowing what it meant. His suspicions were right though, it was skin to skin contact that caused it and not just hand to hand.

Her eyes were large and wide when they reached his. He grinned at her, "Of course I'd teach you." Her eyes twinkled and that rare smile of hers appeared.

He let go, stopping the feeling of being emptied, except this time, it wasn't as deep as it was the last time. He laughed a bit because she still sat there eagerly.

"In the morning Eva. We can start then."

"Really?"

"Yes," he chuckled. "Now, let me rest. I'm assuming it's still the middle of the night?"

She looked down and nodded her head.

"Night Eva."

"Good night Jace." She got down off the bed taking the book with her. She walked over to the door, looking over her shoulder at him with obvious joy on her face. He would do anything to continue to see that look on her face.

She gave a little wave and shut the door behind her as she left. He didn't know what he was getting himself into, but he did feel like it was going to be fun sparing with Eva. He'll find out tomorrow.

Chapter 10
Sparring

"Just as a reminder, your son is turning twelve tomorrow," his wife's voice drifted over to him. Kalvin was relaxing outside for afternoon tea with the love of his life. She was his sunshine, even during the Great War. He feared for his family and without his mother's vision, he would have lost them.

For now, there was no threat, so his family rejoined him just two years ago. He hadn't realized how much he missed in his children's lives and any little thing, even a birthday, was a big event to Kalvin.

"He's practically a man now. When did that happen?" he chuckled at the joy he felt for his son. Jace was exceptional. Kalvin's mother insisted that he must live. She was clear on that when she had her vision so long ago that caused him to spend six years apart from his family. He wished that his mother was still alive to try and get more details from her.

"I suspect that you will be throwing a celebration. Probably inviting the whole town and villagers?" His wife looked over at him with her perfect brow raised.

"You know me so well darling." He looked out across the yard seeing his two daughters down at the pond feeding some ducks. Ms. Kelfer was close by monitoring them. He scanned the grounds and realized he didn't see Jace. Nor did he see Eva their ward. "Where is our son anyway?"

"Oh, probably off at the practice field."

"Practice field? Just like his old man. I wanted to be the best fighter in the land."

"And you are dear."

"Is Eva with him then?"

"Yes. It's surprising really. I have not heard her speak a word these last few months she's been with us. But I've noticed she had taken a liking to Jace. I've seen those lips of hers move when she is near him, which I suspect that she's comfortable with our son to talk with him. Children usually trust their own before they will trust an adult."

"Especially what she experienced before coming here, I don't blame her. However," he stood and took the few steps to his wife, "I still should make sure they aren't getting into trouble." He bent down and kissed his wife on the cheek.

"Alright dear." He winked at his wife which got her chuckling, and he started toward the practice field.

The field was set up to help the men gain strength and work on their fighting technique. Kalvin still held training for the men of the stronghold. He was not able to do that every day, since the men were needed to rebuild the town, but at least twice a week he held the training and usually a good number came out and practiced. They would have time for more once the damage to the wall has been fixed.

As he rounded the corner of his home, he heard the distinct sounds of wooden swords hitting each other or the practice dummies. He was close enough that he could see the outline of two figures. He noticed as he closed in that they were quite a pair.

His son was getting tall, but he still hadn't acquired the muscle, so he looked slightly lanky. Eva on the other hand was small and lithe. She looked like a child compared to his son. He would soon find out why his son would use Eva as a sparring partner.

Kalvin did not want to interrupt them, so he stayed just outside the field and watched. He overheard his son speaking with Eva.

"Now, we've been working on only defensive maneuvers, and you have done quite well with those. But well, isn't going to cut it. You must be exceptional. I feel that knowing some of the attack maneuvers might help you know how to avoid them. You have seen several, but there are others."

His son showed Eva a series of attacks on the dummy. Kalvin smirked and swelled with pride at his son's execution of the moves. They were precise and perfectly done. He would have to remember to show him a few more moves and have Jace spar with him. He knew his son still had much to learn from him in the art of fighting.

His son turned toward Eva and slowly showed each move to her. It looked like she was taking in each arc and line the wooden sword. Her look was calculating and intense.

"Now," his son's voice rang out authoritatively. "I know you know how these attacks look, but I still don't want you trying to use them just yet. Think on the defensive for now. Get ready."

She bent her knees and brought her own sword up. She had a small wooden dagger in her other hand. Interesting choice, Kalvin thought. Why not a shield?

His son raised his own wooden sword in front but had nothing in his other hand. The two stood there for about thirty seconds before his son made an explosive move toward Eva.

Kalvin almost went to shout but he stopped as soon as he realized that Eva had already side-stepped the incoming sword thrust. If he had blinked, he would have missed it.

His son clearly knew that she would do that and went to swing his sword out to try and catch her in the side. Her sword came up to block as she took another series of steps to make space.

His son's smile was evidence that he was pleased with Eva's response. He didn't give her much time to recover because he was on the attack once again. Kalvin was mesmerized at the quickness of both Jace and Eva. Her small frame allowed her to be a smaller target and harder to hit. She was using that to her advantage.

She got herself into a position that she was unable to block with her sword, but she was able to use the dagger to redirect Jace's attack and move out and behind him. It was a clear kill shot and she must have known since she went to strike.

Kalvin thought his son's pride was about to be wounded until he moved expertly blocking her intended strike and then also in the movement ended up behind her with a practice dagger against her throat. Where did he get that from?

"You put too much in the strike and left yourself become vulnerable. You should have brought your dagger up."

Kalvin thought she would show defeat, however she turned her head and she spoke to Jace. Of course, the words were too soft for him to hear but his son heard, and he shook his head. As they separated that is when Kalvin noticed where her dagger had been pointing. She would have had her knife in his son's stomach if it was a real one.

"If I was a big behemoth of a man that might not slow me down. So even though it was a good move, you could have been killed and I could have walked away with a flesh wound. Be defensive first. Only strike when the enemy cannot strike you back. Never assume they do not have a second weapon. Always think they do."

Eva nodded her head and went in a fighting stance once again. Kalvin watched the two for another two rounds before interrupting them.

"So, is this where the two of you ran off to?"

"Father," he quickly stood at attention and turned his gaze down in respect.

"And what pray tell are you doing?" He looked back and forth between the two of them. Eva looked square at him, her stare assessing. Interesting.

"I know it's not normal, but Eva wanted to learn. I didn't think to ask you if it would be permissible."

"Yes, I can see that. But before you think that you would be in trouble for this, why did you see the need for her to have this training?"

"Sir, she made a case that her survival and well-being depended on how strong she was. She fears that she would not be able to escape her attacker if she did not have the necessary skills to do so."

"And you felt this was a valid reason?"

"She brought up the fact that she might not be always protected. I tried to reassure her that we would do that, but she insisted that wasn't enough reason not to know."

"I should be upset," he turned toward Eva, noticed that she had turned her gaze down in defeat. How could he deny this girl these skills? She had already been taken once and kept in a tower for Fate knows how long. As much as he wished to stop this, he wasn't going to. "But I can just overlook and ignore what goes on in the practice field if you two are out here."

His son raised his gaze and smiled. He quickly lowered it but still had the smirk on his face, knowing he won.

"For now, she will not be allowed to join on training days. And do not tell your mother I'm allowing this, deal?"

"Deal," his son looked over at Eva and winked at her. Kalvin noticed she shook her head a tiny bit and rolled her eyes at his son's gesture. Kalvin should keep a close eye on these two, but he would think on that later.

"I do have to interrupt your practice to ask you a few questions Jace, in my study of course."

"Yes father."

"Eva, you can stay and continue to work on your moves if you like, or you can certainly join Sasha and Sonya at the pond." Eva nodded her head. "Alright son, let's get moving."

He started walking toward the exit of the practice field. His son walked over toward the rack of practice equipment and replaced the sword and dagger he had. He jogged over to Kalvin. Before he exited with him, his son turned toward Eva and gave her a small wave and she waved back.

Kalvin placed an arm on his son's shoulders and steered him toward the house. "Let's go discuss what's happening tomorrow, shall we?"

Chapter 11
Missed Celebrations

Jace was a bit wound up to sleep. His father talked about throwing a birthday party for him. It was going to be huge! He was inviting all the townspeople and villagers. He already started to see the evidence around the house where decorations were being placed. The yard was also being set-up with various games, tables, and chairs.

He loved that his father did these little gestures. He didn't care if he celebrated or not, it must have been the years when they were in hiding when parties didn't happen. Now that he was home, safe with his family, these parties happened a lot. Every birthday and holiday were celebrated and the whole stronghold was invited.

As he was lying there in bed, he was thinking about what his father might give him as a present. His sisters would probably give him something, like last year they gave him a picture they drew together. He was so blessed to have a wonderful, giving family. It made him feel special.

His door creaked opened across the room and his gaze quickly darted in that direction. He smirked at the familiar figure that made her way in. He didn't say anything, just watched her reach the edge of his bed, pull out the stool, and climbed up on the bed. She made her way over to her usual sitting spot next to him. She sat there a moment, just looking out at the windows.

"Eva." She didn't even flinch, like she knew that he was awake. He slowly rose and leaned against the headboard with her. "What's up?"

"There was a lot going on today."

"Yeah?"

"First, I thought we'd be in trouble with your father, but it seemed he was okay with it for now."

"Even if he wasn't okay with it, we would have still practiced."

"And then, there was all this activity going on around the house and on the lawn." She turned and looked at him with that tilt in head and asked, "What's everyone doing?"

"Getting ready for a party."

"What's a party?"

"It's a celebration. Sometimes it's celebrating someone's achievements. We could celebrate a holiday, so that's traditional usually."

"So, what are we celebrating?"

"Well, my birthday." She blinked at him a few times. She scrunched her brow, her thinking look.

"What is that?"

"You don't know what a birthday is?" She shook her head side to side. "It's celebrating the day the person was born. Tomorrow is the day I was born twelve years ago."

"Did you do something special?"

"No."

"Then why is there a celebration?"

"Because I'm turning twelve."

"That's not a valid reason."

"Geez. You're making it sound like we shouldn't have a party."

"I just don't understand."

"It's an accomplishment for young people like us that we made it another year. We are the future of this country, and it is important for children to stay alive." She nodded her head, letting the information sink in.

"Alright," she made her conclusion. "You are allowed to have a party." He smiled at her. He wondered if she did that at times to be funny. He would have to work with her on how to tell a joke.

"Anyway, it's going to be real busy tomorrow, so we probably won't be training nor doing any reading. We'll have to postpone that until the next day."

"That's fine. I am rather interested in learning what a party is."

"Yes, a fine learning opportunity," he chuckled. She was too serious for her own good. "And of course, I will probably receive presents."

"What are those?" she asked. Jace looked at her as she sat there patiently. He gestured toward the various items he had in his room.

"It's when another person gives an item to another. All those were gifts, mostly from my family members. I didn't have to purchase them. They were given to me."

"Like Gene did."

"Gene? Who's Gene?" Jace had never heard Eva talk about anyone else. Whose was Gene? He was a tad bit jealous.

"Gene Newly. He was one of the men who found me at the tower. When we reached Holds Stronghold, he purchased clothing for me. I didn't purchase those and based on your description that was a gift from Gene?"

"I guess you could look at it that way."

"Well, that was nice of him. I didn't do anything to deserve those gifts. How can I repay him?"

"I would think in Mr. Newly's situation, he doesn't want to be repaid. I would have done the same thing and would expect nothing in return."

"Maybe I can repay him some day. Even give him a gift in return."

"That sounds like a good idea. Anyway, presents are gifts that are wrapped up, so you don't know what you are getting until you open it."

"Like a surprise?"

"Exactly like a surprise."

"I see." He looked over at Eva, sitting there with that scrunched brow of hers. She was deep in thought.

"Have you ever celebrated a birthday, Eva?" He wasn't going to ask but he was intensely curious.

"I don't remember. I'm going to say no."

"Do you even know when you were born?" She shrugged her shoulders and shook her head side to side. "How are we going to celebrate your birthday if we don't know what day it is?"

"I guess we just don't."

"Well, that is not acceptable. You must experience a birthday party. It is a must in one's lifetime." She just shrugged like it wasn't a big deal. Well, it was a big deal to Jace. He wanted to give her a present, see her face light up in surprise.

He got a spark of an idea. Yes, that just might work. He had to think about his idea, and it would be much easier if Eva were not in the room.

"I'll go back to my room so you can get some sleep." Oh, that was quick.

"Okay. Was there anything else you wanted to talk about?" She moved back to the edge of the bed and climbed down.

"No."

"Alright, I'll see you in the morning."

"See you." She gave a small wave and left his room, closing the door behind her.

Now it was time to get his plan into action. He didn't know how it was going to work, but he was determined that it went well. It was time to start brainstorming.

Chapter 12
Birthday Party

She had never experienced anything like it. Eva wound her way through all the people that appeared for Jace's birthday party. There were so many. Some were playing games on the lawn and others were sitting around drinking and talking, still others just milled around or were sitting at the tables enjoying a small meal.

She wasn't sure how to handle it. She was dealing with a lot of people with a lot of different auras. As she looked from person to person, each one she knew that they were not the auras she'd seen in her years at the tower. She had never seen a rainbow of color like she saw today.

It was also fascinating seeing other children about as well. She was too shy to approach them. Usually, she just stood off to the side watching.

Jace had been around. He seemed to not stay in one place. It sounded like from the conversations that something was about to happen soon. She thought it had to do something with the table set up that had presents on top. She guessed people liked watching others open the gifts they got them.

Eva realized then that she didn't have a gift to give to Jace. What was she going to give him? She had to think of something. She wandered off toward the practice field trying to think of something along the way. If she was in a place where no one was, she would be able to think better. She was in luck that there was not a single soul on the field.

She sat there in the middle of the field with her legs crossed and closed her eyes. She wanted to give him something that he wouldn't expect, something that was special to her and that he would understand and cherish the gift. But what could she give him? She didn't have much time and she didn't have much to give.

She did have one thing, the only thing she could give. She hurried inside to get her gift ready. She needed to find something to wrap it in as well. She made her way to her room. As she got her gift ready, she remembered the nightgown she had accidently ripped one night. She did not tell Lady Jebrow how that happened.

She got the damaged nightgown and tore off a small square. It was the perfect size for her gift. She placed the item in the cloth and folded it. Then she placed it in the pocket on her dress and headed back outside.

Eva hoped that Jace liked her gift. She wouldn't know until he opened it. It looked like there was a flourish of activity going on next to the table where the presents were. She made her way over and was able to move through the crowd until she reached the front to see what was going on.

Jace stood there while his father spoke. "Thank you all for joining my family today in celebration of my son Jace's birthday." The crowd clapped and cheered. Mr. Jebrow raised his hands to quiet the people. "I believe you all have been having a wonderful time and my son wished to open his presents first before we all enjoy a deliciously made dessert our expert baker has prepared. Jace?" He indicated for his son to commence with the gift opening.

Jace smiled and went over to the table and picked up the first present. He unwrapped the gift and took out the item. It was an expertly crafted sword. His eyes got large, and a huge smile appeared on his face. He obviously was impressed with the sword.

"Happy birthday son," Mr. Jebrow called out.

"Thanks dad." He took a couple practice swings and a few people who were close took a step back.

"Might not do that close to people there, son," his father chuckled. Most others laughed along with him.

Jace continued to open gifts and thank each person for them. He was down to the last gift besides hers that she held in her pocket. He lifted the gift off the table and held it in his hands.

"I would like everyone's attention please," Jace called out. Most everyone was already paying attention, but a few others looked his way. "I would like to thank everyone for being here to celebrate the day of my birth. Most of us grew up in homes and were reminded of our birthdays by loved ones. Not everyone grew-up like that though."

Eva didn't know where Jace was going with his little speech, but he had to have been aware of the people around him nodding in understanding.

He continued, "So, I would like to share my birthday with someone, so that she will know that when it's my birthday, it's her birthday too." His eyes found hers and locked on. Oh my, he was talking about her! "Eva, this present is for you." He held out the item in his hand.

It was like everything around her fell away and it was just her and Jace. She slowly made her way toward him, and he stood there waiting for her with a smile on his face. As soon as she reached him, he handed her the present.

She looked down at the wrapped gift in her hand, not knowing what he could have gotten her. "Open it," she heard him whisper at her. She started to open it slowly and carefully. She never had a present before and she wanted to remember every detail. Once the packaging was clear she inhaled at what lay in her hands.

It was a dagger. A real one, not a wooden one like in the practice field. The handle was smooth and had a setting of glimmering stones at the hilt. It was beautiful. She looked up at Jace and looked into his wonderful blue-green eyes. She didn't know how to respond to such a gift.

"Do you like it?" he asked softly. She nodded her head a tiny bit.

"Oh Mayor! I don't know if it's a good idea for two younglings to have sharp objects around your house. I see many accidents in the future!" one of the townspeople shouted out. Others joined in with laughter. All Eva was interested in was Jace.

"Well, I guess I brought that upon myself," Mr. Jebrow responded. "Let's continue the celebration of Jace and Eva's birthday with dessert." The crowd cheered in response and the group of people surrounding the gift table was moving away.

Eva still stood there staring at Jace. He stared right back, waiting with a small smile on his face. She should give him his gift. She looked down a moment to pull her carefully wrapped gift and handed it to Jace. His brow scrunched as he took the small present from her.

"What's this?"

"A present, for you," she said for his ears only.

"For me? Is this from you?" She nodded her head in response. His smile grew even larger. He took the cloth and unfolded it. He lifted out what was hidden inside. It was a braided lock of her hair.

"Eva, I don't know what to say." It was probably a stupid gift. Here she got a dagger and all she could give was her hair. She couldn't have imagined hearing the next words he spoke. "This is the best gift anyone has ever given me."

"What?" She was confused. How was it the best gift? He stepped up to her and took her hand. He knew that they both would feel that strange tug and pull that happened anytime their skin touched, but he did it anyway.

"You gave me a piece of yourself. I will always cherish you. And if I do have to leave, I won't be without you, since a piece will always be near me." He took the braid and placed it in his vest pocket right by his heart.

This foreign feeling welled up inside her. She didn't know what it was, but it consumed every part of her. She felt her Spark pulse as if releasing whatever built up. She realized that whatever she did traveled over to Jace because his eyes grew wide, and he sucked in a breath. They stared at each other for another second before they both let go of each other's hand.

"Wow. That was, different." He shook his head to clear it. "Let's go have some of *our* birthday dessert, shall we?" He directed his hand toward the crowded area on the other side of the lawn.

She might as well. She nodded her head in response and they both made their way over. She knew then and there that she would do anything for Jace. Eva was connected to him, even though she didn't know it at the time. Their lives would forever be changed.

Chapter 13
Panic

"Jace." He felt a small nudge on his shoulder. He was getting used to her coming in the middle of the night, waking him up. She always had some question or another. Eva usually didn't stay long. He didn't startle from it like the first few times.

He rubbed the sleep out of his eyes and saw that she was standing next to the bed. As he was sitting up, he got a feeling that something wasn't quite right. She waited for him to light the candle on the bedside table. Once he did, he saw her large hazel eyes staring at him in panic.

"What's wrong?" he asked, climbing off the bed to assess her himself.

"I'm hurt," she said in a shaky voice.

"Where?"

She looked down and he could see that her brow was scrunched. She mumbled something but didn't quite hear what she said.

"Where did you say?"

"Inside me." Well, that was new to him. In the back of his mind, he did remember reading something about internal wounds, but they hadn't done anything that would cause her to incur that type of injury.

"Okay. I'm not sure what I can do for that. But my mother might know something," he shrugged. He had to guess that maybe his mother would know what was going on. It seemed like when he and his sisters were growing up his mother would be able to know exactly what they needed, from small stitches to herbal remedies. She was the go-to person for all things healing related.

"Come on, I'll take you to her." He led the way out the door and down the hall. They reached his father's bedroom and opened the door. He looked back and motioned for Eva to follow him into the room. He made it to the side of the bed he knew his mother would be on.

"Mother," he said in a whisper. He didn't want to wake his father. She didn't respond to his whisper. This time he did what Eva usually does to wake him up. He nudged his mother's shoulder.

"Mother," he said a little louder. His mother moaned in her sleep. He attempted it again, nudging her and saying her name, "Mother." He saw his mother open her eyes and blinked a few times to see who was waking her.

"Jace? What's the matter sweetie?" His mother yawned and rubbed the sleep out of her eyes.

"Eva says she is hurt."

"Eva?" His mother began to sit up and look around him where she noticed that Eva was there just behind him.

"Yes. She came to me and said that she is hurt on the inside."

"Inside? What do you mean?"

"I'm not sure. She might be talking about an internal wound." His mother raised an eyebrow as she finally stood up out of bed. She made her way to a chair where a robe was draped. She put it on and came back over to them.

"Let's go over to my room. We don't want to wake your father." She ushered them to the adjoining room. Once inside, she closed the door and went over to a small table and lit a candle.

"Now," his mother continued, "Tell me again what is going on?"

Jace sighed and began telling his mother again that Eva came to his room and what she had said.

"Is she bleeding anywhere?"

Jace looked over at Eva waiting to see if she was going to respond. Her eyes still had that panic look in them as she nodded her head to say that she was bleeding.

"She said yes." Jace was starting to become increasingly worried about Eva.

"Is her stomach hurting?"

"Eva," he turned to her, "Is your stomach hurting?" Eva blinked a few times and she slowly started to nod her head. Jace turned his gaze quickly back to his mother.

"What does that mean? Will she be alright? That's not good if she's bleeding inside." His mother turned her gaze toward Eva, her face in contemplation. It didn't take long until his mother's eyes lit up and a smile formed on her face. Why she was smiling, Jace didn't know. "Do you know what's wrong mother? Can you help her?"

"Of course, I can help her sweetie." She came over to him and placed her hand on his shoulder. "However, I need to see to her alone." He started shaking his head before she even finished. He was not going to leave Eva. "I don't care if you don't want to leave, you must."

"But —"

"No buts." She steered him toward the door and opened it. "She's in good hands. Trust me this is a matter that requires delicacy. Go back to bed."

"I won't be able to sleep knowing that she could be hurt." His mother's gaze softened, and she looked between Eva and him.

"I'll make you a promise." He looked up into his mother's eyes. She had always been a source of comfort when he was sick or had bumps and scrapes. "If it is a life-threatening situation, I will come and get you. If you don't see me in the next half an hour, then she is fine. Go to sleep and know that she will be here in the morning."

His mother was not going to let him stay. He didn't know what was going on with Eva, but he wasn't going to try and push his mother's limits.

"I accept your promise."

"Now, run along back to your room sweetie." He turned to leave but took one last look over his shoulder at Eva. She stood there with her hands twisted in front of her. He wanted to go over there and sooth her worry.

His mother was persistent on him leaving and soon he found himself in the hallway with her door shut behind him. Jace looked at the door and resigned to do his mother's biding. He'd go to bed, but he already knew that he would not sleep. He'd wait for Eva.

He pulled out the piece of cloth in his breast pocket of his pajamas and unfolded it. He lifted Eva's braided lock of hair and curled it up into his fist. He began walking toward his room all the while praying that she was going to be fine.

Chapter 14
Summoned

He breathed in the crisp scent of flowers as he walked across the yard. Kalvin could see his daughters catching butterflies and his wife was lounging in a chair with a book in her lap. He saw his son in the distance near the pond. He was just leaning against the tree kicking at nothing.

Kalvin held in his hand a piece of paper that would change this happy family setting. He reached his wife, and she must have heard him coming because she tilted her head up at him. He bent down and gave her a quick peck and took up the chair next to her.

"How's it going?" he asked his lovely wife.

"Oh, just fine."

"You seem tired."

"You have no idea," she said with a huff. He smiled at his beloved and looked out and spotted Jace sulking.

"Do you know what is going on with our son?"

"I'm sure it has to do with what happened last night."

"What happened last night?"

"Let's just say, that he didn't like that I sent him to bed and now he can't spend time with Eva for a few days."

"Eva?" He looked around and that's when he noticed that she wasn't out there. "Is there something wrong with Eva?"

"No dear. She is just experiencing what every young woman experiences."

"Huh?" He was unsure what his wife was talking about.

"She is older than we've originally thought. She is at least Jace's age. She just didn't seem that old because she came to us so malnourished."

"Speak plainly woman. I can't make sense of what you are talking about."

"Eva had her first cycle last night. She is a woman now." Oh. That was unexpected.

"And that is why Jace is upset?"

"Yes, I wouldn't let him stay with her and I couldn't very well explain to him why he couldn't. And then this morning when I told him that she would be in her room for the next few days, he was close to just barging in on her. Of course, I had to give him my stern look and when he asked why," she sighed, "I couldn't tell him what was really going on. The look on his face almost made me cave."

He looked over at his son, still moping around, kicking at nothing. He obviously was still upset about what was going on with Eva.

"And this was what you were doing last night?"

"Eva went to Jace to tell him she wasn't feeling well and then they came and woke me up. After a few questions I guessed what the problem was and was thankful that it was just what it was. Why I am so tired is from all the questions Eva asked me."

"She talked with you?"

"Yes, she did. I don't know why she would want to know everything right at that moment, but I had to finally tell her that we would have to talk about it tomorrow."

He chuckled at his wife. She didn't have much to complain about these days. He thought about the news he held in his hand. His wife would have more to complain about than normal.

"You will have a talk with your son?"

"About what?" his brow scrunched.

"You know. What a father talks to his son about when he becomes a man? I think it's necessary now."

"And why is that?"

"Have you been blind the last few months?" He must have been because he had no idea what his wife was talking about. She must have seen his bemused look. She sighed, "Have you noticed Jace and Eva became very close? I am okay with them having a close *friendly* bond. We don't need them to be anything beyond that right now."

"I don't think that will be a problem."

"How can you be so sure?"

"Because of this." Kalvin held the piece of paper out to her. She had a confused look on her face but took the folded letter. He watched her open it and began to read.

She sucked in a breath and held her hand in front of her mouth. Small tears were starting to form in the corner of her eyes.

"When?" she asked in a shaky voice.

"In a week." That was all the time they had until Jace had to be sent away. Of course, Kalvin didn't want to do it, but a lot was at stake if Jace was not sent to Lous School for Boys. And that tyrant Brosch made that painfully aware in the letter what would happen if he chose to disobey this direct command.

Kalvin stood and went over to his wife. He took her hand and squeezed it, reassuring her that everything will work out in the end.

"I'll go have a talk with our son."

Chapter 15
Unleashed

It had been three days since his father told him that he would be leaving the stronghold. At first Jace was upset that his father would allow this to happen but after reading the letter could he risk the possible destruction of his father's people? The answer was simple, no, he couldn't. It was difficult to take the news and the preparations for his departure have been an ominous foretelling.

He stood next to his bedroom window looking out upon the back lawn. The darkness of the night shadowed some of his favorite areas he liked during the day. He was going to miss everything about his home. He will especially miss one person the most.

The bedroom door squeaked open, and he couldn't help but smile knowing exactly who entered. Eva appeared at his side also gazing out the window as he was.

He turned to her and asked, "How are you?"

"I'm okay," she answered still looking out the window.

"You sure? I haven't seen you in days."

"Yes," she sighed and continued, "Supposedly what I was experiencing is a normal thing."

"I don't get how bleeding internally is normal at any point in time."

"Your mother said you wouldn't get it because it's a female issue."

He raised an eyebrow and asked, "So, you're saying my mother has this female issue as well?"

"Yes." Huh. He hadn't heard about this before. "And I get to experience it once a month."

"Seriously?"

"Trust me. I'm not looking forward to it." She said it with such a straight serious face that he couldn't help but laugh. He was still laughing as she gave him a raised eyebrow. But it was worth seeing the corners of her mouth lift into a soft smile.

This was what he was going to miss, spending time with Eva, even her impromptu nightly visits. How was he going to tell her? As he was thinking about how to start the conversation, she grabbed his hand. He was surprised that she would initiate the contact since each time they touched was never the same. This time was like the last, where he got a feeling of hope. It made him smile at such a thought.

"Come with me, I'd like to show you something," she said and started tugging him toward the door. He followed her, easily keeping up with her shorter strides. They made their way down the stairs and through the kitchen to a door that led outside. She hurried across the dark yard toward the wall. Set inside the wall was a door. He wouldn't have known it was there unless he was shown it.

Eva pressed against it, and they exited the confines of the stronghold. She hurried to the remnants of a stone structure; it could have been a villager's home before the Great War. They passed under the small arch into the middle and what Jace saw stopped him in his tracks.

The movement caused her to stop and look back at him. She must have realized his look of awe, because she gave a brilliant smile and released his hand to continue forward. The floor of the structure was blanketed with glowing flowers. They were so ethereal. He watched her make her way among them, reaching out her hands and grazing her fingers along the soft pedals.

She turned back toward him and spread her arms wide, "What do you think?"

He was speechless. The small area she stood in was bathed in moonlight since the roof had long ago caved in. She looked like a moon fairy from a children's story he heard when he was younger. He was tempted to believe such beings existed.

Jace slowly made his way among the small glowing buds and lightly touched them as if studying something rare and precious. "What are they?"

"I'm not sure. I've been searching in the library but I'm not a quick reader yet." She looked down at her toes while she fidgeted with her hands in front of her.

"I have no doubt you'll find the answer soon. They seem so, magical."

"They are only like this when the sky is clear, and the moon's light is directly on them. I think in the day light they look like a regular flower."

"How'd you know about them?" He watched her move off toward one side of the structure where the wall was crumbled. She sat down on the ledge looking out across the plains beyond.

"I found them."

"But how? When?" He made his way over to her and sat down next to her.

She turned to him and smiled that sweet smile of hers. "At night. I wander around and explore. That's how I found the hidden door in the wall and this place."

"That's taking a big risk coming out here by yourself."

"Don't worry," he heard the familiar ting of metal and a dagger appeared in her hand, "I come prepared."

He had to chuckle at that. She probably knew enough now from the training to at least maim and escape.

Jace's expression grew serious as he thought about what would happen in less than a week. No more adventures with Eva. When she discovered new things, it was exciting to see the wonder in her eyes. Like tonight, she brought that wonder and excitement to him just by showing him these glowing flowers.

"What is it?" she asked, seeing his saddening expression.

"I don't want to tell you."

"Why not?"

"Because you're not going to like it." She scooted closer to him and took his hand and placed it in hers. She threaded their fingers together and looked up into his eyes.

"Even so. Tell me, please?"

He took a steadying breath and told her of the requirements that Brosch set in place for all sons of prominent figures in Hockland to be sent at the age of twelve to the Lous School for Boys. Eva glanced down at their locked hands with a frown. He could feel her emotions going all over the place.

"I will be leaving within the week to fulfill this requirement." She took her hand away, but not before he felt this feeling of intense anger. She started walking out into the plains away from him. "Eva, wait!" he called to her.

Jace got down and started to go after her. She took off in a run and when she was almost to a grouping of trees she fell to her knees. Just before reaching her, he saw her look up at the sky, screamed and then he was thrown back by a force.

Jace was startled, not sure where it came from. He sat up and looked in Eva's direction. She seemed to not be affected, so he stood and approached her bent form. As he closed in, he noticed everything was flattened in a circle surrounding Eva. Was she the source of that force?

He slowly approached and heard her soft cries. He knelt in front of her and gathered her up in his arms. He never heard her cry before, and his heart was breaking.

Chapter 16
Bittersweet Goodbye

"You can't go," she said between her sobs. Eva's body was shaking uncontrollably. She didn't know what she just did, except that whatever she did made her slightly weak. All this anger came roaring to the surface, and she had to get away. She had a strong sense that she was going to hurt Jace if he was right next to her.

His arms felt like a warm jacket. She'd seen Sasha and Sonya do this many times with others, but Eva never experienced it herself. She didn't know that she would gain this comforting warm feeling from this kind of touching. She slowly brought her own arms up and held onto Jace with the same fierceness he was holding her.

"Don't you see? If I don't go something bad will happen. I wish I could stay. I really do, but I can't. You understand, don't you?"

At that moment she was transported into a time and place in the future, a future if Jace did not leave to attend this school.

The shops in the stronghold were ablaze and the townspeople were running to get away. The men who had gone through training tried to fight and protect their town, but they were no match for Brosch's cronies. The vision moved toward the Jebrow home, where a young girl, Sasha, was being dragged away crying and screaming. Just inside the door lay a prone figure. As Eva came closer, the eyes of Jace's dead sister stared up at her.

She blinked and was back in Jace's embrace in the open fields outside the stronghold. She knew what would happen if he stayed. Tragedy would strike. She knew that he wouldn't risk losing any of his family.

"I do," she softly responded. Her vision was clear on the outcome if he didn't leave. And so, he must go, even though the separation would feel like her Spark was leaving her. He pulled back from her and tilted her chin up, so they were looking into each other's eyes.

"I'm willing to sacrifice myself if it means saving the people I love." He reached up and tucked her hair behind her ear. He gave her such warmth and hope. He had always eased her Spark with just a single touch. Even after her apparent surrender to her rage and subsequent explosion, he was there comforting her. He should have been afraid of what she did; instead, he still came near her.

"I don't want you to die."

"I don't want to die either. And since they are sending me to a school, I don't think they are sending me there to be killed. If it only means that I must be away for a while and possibly feel a little lonely, then I think I can handle that if it means saving others."

"I want to come with you." He smiled down at her brushing his thumb across her cheek.

"You can't come with me in person." She closed her eyes trying to hold back the sudden urge to cry. Jace continued, "However, you did give me something to remember you by." She opened her eyes and saw that he had pulled out the lock of hair that she gave him. "And whenever I hold this, I will be thinking of you Eva. This will give me strength and hope. Hope that I will make my way back to my home, and to you."

She knew that something inside her would always be tied to Jace. She would be able to feel his presence even from far away. The problem was not knowing. She wouldn't know what he was doing or when he'd be back and that was the scariest part of the whole thing.

He rested his forehead against hers and sighed. They stayed like that for several minutes, taking comfort in each other's arms through their bond.

"Promise you'll be waiting for me," he said softly. Eva pulled away and looked up into his uncertain eyes.

"Always." He gave her one of his small smiles that melted her heart.

"Come on. We should get back home before someone notices we are missing." He stood and held out a hand to help her stand. She grasped his hand and used him as leverage to lift herself off the ground.

She brushed off the front of her nightgown where there were two obvious knee prints. Lady Jebrow is going to wonder where those came from.

They traveled back through the magical place where now the flowers were not so bright because the moon had made its way behind some clouds. They didn't speak as they made their way to the hidden door and back into the house through the kitchen.

This time they went past his room to the room that she was given. He led her inside and stopped in the middle of the room.

He dropped her hand, and their connection was immediately severed. She was not happy that she wouldn't be able to feel him like this when he was gone.

"Don't look so glum. You still have me for a few days yet."

"The outcome will still be the same in a few days. You'll be gone."

"Not for long. At least, I hope it won't be for long."

"Then I'll be waiting," she gave him a small smile trying to believe that everything will turn out for the best.

"I wouldn't expect anything less. Night Eva." He walked out the door turning just slightly to look back at her as the door was shut slowly.

"Good night Jace." She will remember those piecing blue-green eyes and brown-blonde hair. She was starting to get the feeling that Jace was a part of her life and had to remain so. She realized that she would wait for him to eternity. She just hoped that wasn't the case.

Chapter 17
Escape

7 years later…

He ran as fast as his feet could carry him. He took the chance that was given to him to get away. He had nothing but the clothes on his back. He didn't remember his own name. He was just a number to them. Number 034 ran past tree branches that seemed to claw at him and slow him down. He had to keep going. His life depended on it.

He heard dogs bark in the distance behind him. That spurred him on like nothing ever could. He stumbled a few times, cutting his feet on jagged stones and sticks. They didn't give his people shoes. Slightly limping he came upon a clearing where a small stone hut stood. He stopped at the edge of the clearing catching his breath. He surveyed the hut and saw a stream of smoke rising from the chimney and a small light glowed from under the door affixed to the front.

The dogs barked again reminding him he didn't have time to rest. The Chasers were getting closer. He chanced it and approached the hut. He knocked on the door and as he waited, looking around anxiously.

The door opened a crack where a hooded figure appeared. The face was obscured since the light illuminated them from behind.

"Why did you knock?" the voice croaked out the question.

"Please, I beg you. I need shelter," he didn't want to be caught out here. He heard what happened when the dogs got a hold of the escapees.

"Shelter. Shelter I can give, but what can you give in return?"

"I, I don't understand. I have no possessions."

"Is that what they've told you?"

"What?" The dogs barked again causing him to look behind him terrified that they would catch him. He turned back to the hooded figure behind the door and pleaded. "I'll give you whatever you want. I'm begging you, please hide me."

He thought that the person wouldn't let him in, but the door opened further, and he took that as admittance and rushed into the hut. He stepped into an open area where a fire was crackling low in the fireplace and a large pot hung over the embers. A table was close by that was covered with various tools and bowls. The ceiling to the right of him had various dried plants hanging.

He heard the door close, and a heavy lock was secured in place. He turned to the hooded figure expectantly.

"Thank you," he whispered, not wanting to be heard if the Chasers were close by.

The hooded figure made their way over to a blanket that was hung over a small round hole that led to a small storage room. The figure moved the material out of the way.

"In here." Number 034 didn't hesitate. He ducked into the storage space and found a spot behind a barrel that would be big enough for him to hide behind. "Stay silent. Do not come out. Whatever you hear, don't come out." The figure dropped the blanket back and he was left in the darkness of the room.

The dogs had reached the clearing and he could hear the mumbling of the Chasers. He heard pounding on the door a moment later. He heard the shuffling of the hooded figure's feet as they made their way to the door. This was it, the moment where he found out if this person would save him or betray him.

Something slid across the door's surface, a look-out hole he'd bet, and the hooded figure spoke. "Why did you knock?"

"We need admittance to search this premises for an escapee," a Chaser answered.

"Admittance. Admittance I can give, but what can you give in return?" Was this person nuts? Weren't those the same questions he was asked?

"What you'll get in return is your life. Open this door and we won't have any problems."

"I don't remember having given that item away for it to be returned to me."

"Stop with the riddles!" the Chaser shouted. "This is your last chance to open this door, or we will use force."

"You have nothing to offer in exchange for entrance. I must decline." With that, Number 034 heard the slot slide back closed.

The dogs barked and then the pounding on the door began. The Chasers were trying to break the door in. He wanted to see what was going on, but he was too afraid that if he moved from his hiding place that he would be spotted.

He heard the hooded figure's voice in a low hum. They were speaking something unintelligible. A tingly feeling washed over his skin. Then suddenly, the pounding stopped along with the dogs barking. He was tempted to look but he remembered the hooded figure said he mustn't come out.

He heard the lock disengage and the door was opened.

"You poor lost souls," the croaked voice of the hooded figure rang out into the darkness. "Let me help you find your way, to damnation."

Number 034 heard a twang of steel and grunts and gurgles. The yipping of dogs sounded like they were running away. All lay quiet for a moment until the door was shut. He didn't hear any shuffling of feet and he desperately wanted to look out.

Several minutes passed and he heard the door open again. Once it was closed the lock was put into place. The shuffling feet came close to the hole and the blanket was lifted, letting a meager amount of light into the tiny space.

"Come, you will exchange your item before you continue on your mission." What in the world was this person talking about? He wasn't on any mission. The only mission he had was to leave that hell hole he came from.

"Mission?" He asked.

"A very special mission it is." The hooded figure moved off toward the table and started to rummage through the supplies. "Have a seat Number 034." He moved over to a chair that was close to the fireplace and lowered himself down.

"How did you know my name?"

"Is it not burned into your skin?" He looked down to the inside of his wrist where the small number showed. He tried tugging at his sleeve to cover his number.

The figure moved with a bowl in their hands over to the large pot hanging in the fireplace. A gnarled hand took a ladle which was dipped into the pot and the liquid was placed into the bowl. The person swirled the liquid, mixing it with what they had placed in there. They made their way over to him and held out the bowl for him to take.

"Drink." He took the bowl and looked at its contents. A lovely aroma wafted up from the bowl. He took a sip. "All of it," the voice croaked out.

He downed the whole bowl, swiping his mouth with the back of his hand. The figure took the bowl from him and placed it back on the table. They turned quickly back with their head bowed down and hands were out, palms up. They started to speak in a low murmur.

He shifted uncomfortably in his seat. He started to feel a tingly feeling along his skin. The hooded figure slowly moved toward him still murmuring unintelligible words. He was too curious with what was going on to realize anything was happening until it was happening.

He grabbed his chest as if a force was trying to leave him. He tried to stand, but the feeling in his chest made him fall to his knees. He was unable to catch his breath. He looked up at the shadowy opening of the hood, trying to make out the face that was doing this to him.

He couldn't stop the gnarled hand that reached out toward him. He felt this sudden release inside him, like something was leaving. There was this mist that went out of his skin, and it floated over to the outstretched hand.

His eyes grew large as he watched the gnarled hand rejuvenate and age spots cleared, and long delicate fingers appeared. The mist traveled over the rest of the figure and once it covered the individual the mist dissipated, and the pressure released from his chest. He took in a huge breath and slumped over as his hands caught himself from hitting the ground.

The delicate hand lifted his chin and his eyes landed on a young woman's face with violet eyes and long white-blonde hair. A smile graced her beautiful face.

"You have fulfilled your obligation with me. We will now need to prepare you for a journey."

"What journey?" he asked, mesmerized by the woman's soft musical voice.

"To seek the One who will save our people."

"Why me?"

"I have seen it."

"You are a Seer?" She nodded her head. As she stood, he rose with her to make sure he followed what she was saying.

"Your journey will take you south. It is essential that you reach the One."

"You speak about the prophesy of the Child?"

She held up a finger and a smirk came across her lips. "The One once was a child but is no longer."

"So, the Child is grown?" The woman nodded. "I still don't understand why I must go."

"You hold knowledge the One needs. You have seen the inner workings of his stronghold. This information the One needs if the prophesy is to take place."

"Will I know the One when I find him?"

"That I cannot foresee." She moved away from him toward a trunk that she quickly opened. She started pulling out clothing and other items. "You cannot delay. You must leave immediately, or the Chasers will catch up with you."

"How will I know that I've reached my destination?" She hurried over and placed the items she dug out in his hands.

"Get dressed. Follow the Point of Aster among the stars. Do not stray from your mission."

Number 034 pulled on the pants and shirt that was given to him. As he was securing footwear to his scarred feet, she busied herself around the small home filling a sack with supplies. As he slipped on a coat she approached with a full sack.

"I still don't understand why it has to be me," he said. She smiled at him and placed a hand against his cheek.

"All will be revealed to you in time." She handed him the sack. "Now go." She pushed him toward the door and out. She raised her hand and proclaimed, "May the Fates led you and the Spark sustain you. Safe journeys Number 034." The door was shut on the small stone hut, and he heard the lock move back into place.

He looked at the door wishing he could ask more questions, but Seers were known to be vague, and he probably wasn't going to be getting any other answers. He slung the sack across his back and glanced up into the night sky. He found the constellation of the warrior Aster holding his spear. The Point of Aster referenced the tip of Aster's spear. He turned himself to face the direction the spear was pointed and started on his journey.

Only Fate made it possible for his escape and he will take that as a sign that he was meant for something greater. He was to help the Child prophesy be realized. The time has come for the tyrant to fall and the people of Hockland pulled out of the darkness.

Chapter 18
Home Again

The sun glared down on him and his horse. He had set off early that day to make it home by evening. His horse nickered and swung its head to avoid the gnats that lingered. He too was getting irritated, and saddle worn. He rubbed the back of his neck to ease the tension. It seemed to not be working.

It has been too long since Jace was allowed to do his own thing. He completed his requirements in attending that dreaded school and now he was making his way back to his family. He closed his eyes against the sun to try and remember the faces of his parents and sisters. And of course, there was one face he most definitely wanted to see.

They probably have all changed and he was coming home as a stranger. He wasn't the lanky teenager any longer. He was a formidable height and size, towering over most at six foot three. His muscles bulged and strained against his clothing. Thank the Fates that he thought of a way to build his strength. Who would have thought cutting down trees and moving logs would be so rewarding?

His horse was lazily trotting along with Jace barely involved with guiding the animal. He sat forward and squinted into the distance. He recognized the old lookout post that was the edge of his father's land.

He smiled at the thought of seeing the people he loved once again. As he moved closer on the horse he wondered if his father had re-staffed this post. It was a slow rebuild from the damage done from the Great War. Did that really happen fifteen years ago?

A movement caught his eye atop the lookout. If he hadn't been looking at it in that moment, he would have missed it. There was someone up there. The lookout was not shaded with trees and with the sun high in the sky it was easy to spot a figure descending the ladder. The person was getting down to probably inspect the unknown traveler. He wasn't even the least bit offended by that.

The person waited for him with arms crossed. Jace couldn't make out who it was, but he didn't seem to recognize the man. Must be one of the village boys all grown up. To not look so opposing and to make sure he didn't seem trapped, he got off his horse. He needed to stretch his legs anyway. He held his horse's reins as he continued down the road closing in on the young man.

Jace saw the man drop his arms to his side and tilt his head. Wait a second. That head tilt looked familiar. The man started to jog towards him. Jace looked behind him to make sure there wasn't anything coming and there wasn't, so the man was running toward him. He wished he had a weapon on him. The man didn't look to have one so Jace figured he could take him out if necessary.

Jace stopped and crouched slightly to anticipate an attack. As the man came closer a swish of long dark hair caught his attention. Wait, that wasn't a man. He was trying to process everything and the contradiction he was seeing of long braided hair and pants caused him to pause slightly.

Right before she launched into his arms hazel eyes connected with his. He caught her against his chest and when just the slightest bit of skin contacted, her arm touching the back of his neck, he knew exactly who it was. The familiar connected feeling he had missed came to life. It was full of joy, promise, faith, and pulsing life to the fullest. It was so much he almost dropped to his knees.

She pulled away from him and a glorious smile was there to greet him.

With his own smile in place and laughter in his eyes he breathed out the only name he was looking forward to saying, "Eva."

"Jace." They stood there a moment taking each other in. Wow, she changed. Even though her attire might be a bit odd, he wouldn't mistake her as a man again. She was all female. She filled out. He remembered how small and skinny she was. She had no definition, just skin and bone. Now, her eyes sparkled and didn't seem as large with full cheeks. His hands were on her waist still and he noticed how shapely she was even though it was impossible to tell with the clothing.

Before he got himself in trouble, he let her go. She grabbed his hand and started pulling him toward the stronghold. "Come on. I'm sure your family would love to see you."

"Hold on," he chuckled and released her hand. The contact was just too much right now. His heart sped up at the touch and he was afraid his heart would burst out of his chest. "At least let me guide my horse." He used that as an excuse.

She didn't seem to be bothered by it. She tilted her head in the stronghold's direction. He pulled his horse along and fell in step next to her.

"What were you doing up in the lookout?" Jace asked.

"Waiting."

"For?" She turned to him and smiled. "Me? You were waiting for me? I hope you haven't been up there every day for the last seven years." She laughed. Oh, it was such a sweet sound to hear.

"No. That would be silly. I just went up there this morning."

"I don't understand. How'd you know I'd be coming?" She shrugged. Oh, keeping secrets? Well, there had to be something behind that shrug. He'd have to ask her later.

They continued for a while just enjoying each other's company. They started to reach the fields and they looked to be prospering.

"We've doubled the output on crops," Eva explained. "We implemented a new system and plant rotation that was favorable."

"That sounds great."

"The animal herds have also doubled in the last three years. That was a little trickier to accomplish, but it seems like we figured that one out."

"Why all the need for more crops and animals? Has the town population increased?" Eva didn't answer right away, and he saw that brow of hers scrunch up.

"I think that was something your father wanted to discuss with you," she finally said.

"But you know why, don't you?" Her mouth twitched as if she was trying to hold back a smile.

"I do. I might have overheard him talking about it."

"Ah. Well, I can't wait to catch up with everyone." They were getting close to the gate entrance. He glanced along down the wall, and it looked like all the repairs had been completed. "Has the wall been fully repaired?"

"It has. I think that was about four years ago."

"Four? Geez I've missed a lot." They walked into the stronghold, and it was thriving. It was very busy with people milling about. What he noticed was how carefree everyone was. It was quite a change to some of the places he went through on his trip back home.

They reached his house shortly and he took a moment at the entrance to look up at the structure. Eva took his horse and passed the reins to a stable hand. He smiled at her and continued up the few steps and into the main entranceway.

His eyes had to adjust to the interior of the room since the glaring sun was left outside. As he adjusted his gaze, he found his father who was talking to one of the servants.

He was glad that he recognized him. He was worried that he wouldn't. His father looked the same except for the graying hair at his temples and the lines at the corner of his eyes. Jace stood there with Eva next to him and waited.

A moment later his father glanced over at them. It took him only a moment, a few blinks and his father's face lit up with joy. He approached him and brought him into a fierce hug.

"Jace."

"Father." They pulled away from each other and his father clapped him on his shoulder.

"Welcome home son."

Chapter 19
Visions

Why wasn't her heart slowing down? It had been rapidly beating ever since she recognized Jace walking down the road. Eva stood watching the exchange between father and son. She knew how much the mayor missed his son. He tried to hide it, at least to his people, but in the confines of his home, it was noticeable.

Jace looked different. Eva noticed he was taller, but she was taller as well. For a woman, she was tall standing at five foot ten. Not very many men she could look up to. Along with his impressive height she noticed how his arms strained against his sleeves. He easily caught her when she decided to jump him. She wasn't expecting to do that, she was just overly excited.

"Why didn't I receive a letter?" the mayor asked his son.

"I would have, but I came home right away after I was dismissed. It was but a few days travel. By the time you did get the letter you would have known only a few hours before I arrived anyway."

The mayor laughed and clapped his son on the back. The two men stood at eye level. The mayor's blue aura brightened, obviously because of the presence of his son. Jace on the other hand, was naked of an aura color as ever.

In all the books she had read over the past several years she still didn't find an answer to that question, why she couldn't see his aura. She at least gained some knowledge about auras and energy in one of the books hidden on the top shelf of the library. She wasn't a small girl anymore and could easily reach those books.

What she learned was that everyone had an energy source called the Spark. This Spark would glow bright or dim depending on what energy level the person was at. It now made sense to Eva why people slept because their Spark was dim and had to be replenished. She couldn't see her own Spark, so she had no idea why she didn't need to sleep. Was it because her Spark never dimmed? That question the book did not answer.

It did answer her questions about the color auras she saw. Everyone had a predisposed level of ability that would be more than others. It showed what the person would be best at based on the person's aura color. For instance, the mayor had a blue aura. He was predisposed to have the ability of strength. Lady Jebrow had a yellow-colored aura. Hers tended to be more golden, but it fell into the yellow family. She was predisposed to beauty. This all made sense to Eva because she could see this ability was more prominent than the rest in each person.

A few questions arose once she started to learn about the Might. These were people that displayed exceptional ability in their predisposed aura. They were able to use their ability to their advantage. If you were to compare the mayor to someone who had the Might with the same aura color and pitted them against each other, the one with Might would eventually win. Eva was sure the mayor would still put up a good fight since his aura was one of the brightest she had seen.

Of course, more questions that she did not have answers to, such as, what is the difference between a dull or bright aura? Is it tied into the Spark when it is dull or bright? It wasn't too hard to remember the guards at the tower where she was found. Each one of them had a dull aura.

"Oh! You're home!" Lady Jebrow squeaked out from the kitchen area spotting Jace. She hurried over to her son, embracing him in a bone-crushing hug.

"Mother," he said in a strained voice.

"It's been too long dear. I prayed that you would return safe and look at you! My how you've grown."

"Thanks, I guess."

"Kalvin," she turned to the mayor, "you do know what this means?" The mayor shrugged in response. "This birthday celebration can be twice as big!"

"Mother, I don't need a party," Jace began but his father shook his head trying to say to just let his mother have her way.

"Oh yes, we were just planning one for Eva, but…Eva! What are you wearing?" All eyes turned to her. All she could do was shrug and try to look innocent. "I thought I've told you not to go traipsing around wearing, whatever it is you are wearing. Go look more presentable." Eva rolled her eyes and started toward the stairs that led to her room.

"Hey Eva," she felt Jace's hand stop her before she started up the stairs. In a low voice he said, "Why don't you meet me on the practice field? I don't mind if you look like that," he winked at her. She smiled and continued to her room. She heard his father's voice drift up towards her as he spoke to his wife.

"Now dear, go get that party underway. I'm sure you have a lot to prepare now. When is it again?"

"Two days! I have two days to try and sort everything out. Don't worry Jace, it will be spectacular!" As Eva reached the top of the stairs, she looked down the banister to see Lady Jebrow marching off toward the kitchen and began giving orders of what she needed done.

"Come," the mayor said to Jace. "We have much to catch up on." They both moved off toward the study where they entered to continue their conversation.

She knew what they were going to be discussing. This country wasn't stable, and it was going to boil over soon. They were close to another war, and nobody wanted that.

But that was concern for another time. She needed to get ready to meet Jace for a long overdue match on the practice field. She hurried to her room and gathered her sword and dagger. Not changing her clothes as Lady Jebrow had wanted, she hurried off toward the servant stairs that led right to a door that went outside. She made her way out this door and over to the practice field.

She figured that she would practice while she waited for the mayor to finish discussing political matters with his son. She made her way out to the middle of the grounds and looked around.

The mayor allowed her to come to the training days he gave. Eva of course was the only woman among the trainees. That didn't bother her so much though since she was better than all of them. She was still building up her strength, but she did find a way around that. She was skilled in evasive maneuvering but was also great at intricate dagger work. She didn't like to boast, but she hadn't meant anyone she couldn't beat.

As she began with a few warm-up exercises, a soft breeze blew through the field. It felt great on her heated skin, being in the sun training had her skin sheen slightly with sweat. She closed her eyes a moment to feel the breeze run across her arms and face. A sudden image appeared to her.

It was of a man. It was like the one she had a few days ago of Jace. This man was traveling on foot. His clothes were ill-fitted and his red hair and bearded face was unkempt. His eyes burned with vengeance. Even in the vision she could see a strong orange aura. However, it was pulsing, like it was alive. She had never seen an aura like that.

The image faded and when she opened her eyes, she was standing in the middle of the practice field. If that vision was like when she saw Jace, knowing in the vision that Jace was thinking of home and her, was the red-haired man thinking of her? All she knew was that she was going to have a visitor real soon.

Chapter 20
Training Hard

After Jace took in the look of his old room and found where he stashed his sword, he made his way to the training area. His father told him some events that were troubling. The reason for the growth in output of crops and animals was because the Brosch Stronghold was demanding that every stronghold give a certain amount to him. This was payment for not taking the town's children and burning down the village.

Jace learned a lot about Brosch's tyranny when at school. The guy was a micro-manager. Jace saw it in the way he was taught certain concepts. Brosch was teaching the next generation to see history through his eyes, which was all distorted and clearly parts were missing. He used threats to get his way. Jace watched as his classmates became mindless drones.

The biggest challenge at the school was not stand out. Brosch had an eye for the talented and exceptional so if any one boy was doing something above the rest, he was closely watched by the professors and if the boy was really showing potential, he was taken. He saw two boys taken during his stay and neither of them came back.

Jace had a sense of what was transpiring and made sure he just stayed average. Oh, he knew all the answers to the questions on tests he took. He purposely answered them incorrectly. He tried to appear weak, but he found a way to gain strength. They didn't allow the boys to practice any fighting and were severally punished if found out. He either practiced when he was out in the woods or in the confines of his room. His roommate never ratted him out.

Now, he was home. He showed those professors he was worth nothing and he wouldn't amount to anything. He deceived them all.

Jace stepped onto the practice field and the wind ruffled his hair. Eva stood in the center facing away from him. She stood unnaturally still. He came up to her and placed a gentle hand on her shoulder.

"Eva?" She seemed to be looking far off and her brow was scrunched. Oh, that was her thinking face. "Something bothering you?" She blinked a few times and shook her head.

"No. It's nothing."

"You can tell me later, since I do know it was more than just nothing." She glanced at him, and a slow smile crept on her face.

"Maybe." She turned and faced him getting prepared by adjusting her grip on her sword and dagger.

"I wasn't asking you." He rolled his shoulders back and readied his sword. She huffed and rolled her eyes.

"You ready?" She asked with a sly smile on her face.

"As ready as I'll ever be." He started to circle her in a crouch. She readied herself by taking careful steps to maximize distance while having her sword in front of her.

He went on the attack, striking right at her center. She expertly dodged the stab and even went so far as to reach out her own sword for a strike. He caught the movement and was able to block her attack. Her dagger came next, swinging up toward his middle. He had to push her away where their swords were locked to move away from her dagger. She was still able to make a slice in his shirt.

He felt the spot and was relieved that she only did get his shirt. "Maybe we should have practiced with the wooden swords," he mumbled.

"Are you saying you're not fast enough?" Her eyes twinkled with mirth.

"No," he squinted at her with his brows drawn down. He took his stance again.

This time she struck out and he blocked and countered with his own swipe to her legs. She somehow was able to jump out of the way, while also reaching out with her sword. He was able to lean back to avoid her attack and then she struck with her dagger.

He was able to use her momentum to pull her toward him, which showed surprise on her face as she tried to release his grip and move away at the same time. She went low to the ground and pulled so that he was now falling toward her.

They both could have used their swords, but of course they were only practicing, and they really didn't want to kill each other. She shoved her legs in his middle and he went flying over and landed on his back. He immediately turned and saw a sword coming down at him. He blocked a few strikes until he was able to push with his sword to make her back up a few steps.

That gave him time to get back to his feet and ready for another strike. He anticipated her moves the same way she was predicting his. He was impressed with how graceful she moved, like floating above the ground her feet were so light.

He was able to bat away the dagger and it went flying away from her, leaving her with only one weapon. She executed the perfect attack that he knew she would do. Using her momentum, she stumbled slightly, and he was able to grab her wrist and pull it behind her. He brought her up against his front and he took his free hand and ran a finger across her neck.

The sensation that came through the contact was electric, almost pleasurable. They both groaned as he finished pretending to drag a dagger across her neck. As soon as the contact ended, he was elbowed in the stomach as he released her.

She was breathing heavily and gave him that famous scrunched brow of hers. "Don't do that," she hissed. He held out his hands and chuckled.

"What? I was just letting you know what could have happened if I had a dagger in my pocket. Don't ever think the enemy only has one weapon."

For her response she charged him and took several swipes where he was able to block and dodge effectively. He got in a position again where he was able to grab her wrist, but as soon as he did, he felt a force push him away and he landed on his backside. He landed hard and when he sat up, he was at least ten feet away from where he started.

Eva hurried over to him and knelt. "I'm sorry. I didn't know what I was thinking." She reached out a hand to help him up.

"Nope. That's fine, I got it." He got to his feet and rolled his neck and shoulders trying to make sure he was all in one piece. "Was that the same thing you did in the field?" She looked around and when she turned back to him, she nodded her head.

"I'm impressed. It felt like I was run over by a bull."

"I've been working to harness it in one direction."

"Well, it was effective." He dusted himself off and looked at Eva as she fidgeted her hands in front of her. "Hey, I'm fine Eva. Don't worry, I can take a few hits."

"That was the first time I've done that on a person so I wasn't sure how it would go. I wasn't meaning to use you as a test."

"Well, the test was successful, believe me." He walked up to her and tilted her head up to meet his eyes. From the brief touch, he felt worry through the link. "I won't tell anyone. Your secret is safe with me," he smiled at her. She gave him a weak one back.

Jace continued, "I believe it's almost time for supper and I'm sure that mother would not want us to show looking like this." He indicated to their dusty clothes and disheveled appearance from fighting. "We should probably get back to the house and wash up." He bent down and retrieved his sword, also retrieving Eva's dagger. He turned to her and held it out for her to take.

"Thanks," she took the dagger and placed it in the sheath at her waist. He led her to the servant door, which he was sure that she used to come out here and opened it. As he watched her make her way over to him, he was entranced with the way she walked. She was confident and held her head high. Every move he took in, from the way she stepped to the swing of her hips.

He had to get himself under control. She walked past him as the door was opened and he could smell her sun-kissed skin. She smelled like fresh air and sunshine. He needed to clear his head. Hopefully a fresh bath would help, because if not, he was bound to embarrass himself.

Chapter 21
Party

Eva sat at the table with some young women from town that were good friends with Sasha and Sonya. She never got involved with making friends. Training and gaining knowledge were her focus.

The birthday party was in full swing, and it looked like everyone was having a good time. Lady Jebrow planned the party in the evening which she said it worked out because young men and women stay up at all hours in the night. Eva did that anyway, so she really didn't get what she was talking about.

Sasha came back over from wherever she went with two drinks in her hand. She set one down in front of Eva.

"There you go," Sasha took her seat and began sipping her drink.

"What is it?" Eva asked.

"An adult beverage of course. Just don't tell my mother I snuck one for myself." Eva took the drink and brought it to her nose. She sniffed and it smelled like berries. She took a small sip and the sweet tasting liquid lit up her taste buds. There was a hint of something else in there, but she didn't know what. That must have been the adult beverage part Sasha mentioned.

Eva sat silently listening to the conversations the women were having around her. They chatted on about boys and marriage and all sorts of things. They even would talk about other people, like who was courting who and about rifts with some people's marriages. It was a gossip fest.

"Everyone, can I have your attention please!" the mayor announced as he stood up on a chair so he could be seen. "Tonight, we celebrate two young people coming of age!" There were shouts and cheers. Obviously, there were several that had a little too many adult beverages already.

The mayor held up his hands to quiet everyone and continued. "I would like to honor my son Jace on this special occasion by presenting him with a gift." Jace had been standing with a group of guys and seemed to be embarrassed that he would be receiving a gift at his age. The mayor pulled a dagger from his side and held it up for all to see. "This dagger belonged to my father. It was crafted by the Wedset mountain people, forged to be the best. I now give it to you Jace. It is tradition that a young man receives the gift of a sword at his coming of age gathering. Since I gave Jace a sword several years ago, this seemed more fitting." The people laughed about the joke.

The mayor got down from his chair and handed Jace the dagger. Jace took it in his hand and looked over it was an appreciative smile. His father gave his son an affection pat on the shoulder and the crowd clapped and cheered for the gift exchange. Jace said something to the mayor, but Eva was too far away and there was too much noise to make out what he said to him.

Jace began moving away as the mayor once again took his stand on the chair. He raised his hands to quiet everyone again. "The other individual I would like to honor tonight is Eva." She stood and walked toward the mayor like Jace had done. She saw many people looking at her, nodding their heads as she passed. "This young woman has faced many trials in her young life, and she overcame those trials and became this beautiful woman you see before you today. Traditionally at a coming-of-age party for a woman, she would be subject to much courting and possible engagement before the night was out."

Eva looked at the mayor with a raised eyebrow. She was very concerned with all this. He continued, "However, if any of you try and ask me for her hand tonight, I will punch you in the face." The crowd's laughter eased Eva's tension and she sighed in relief. "For Eva, we will just celebrate that she made it to adulthood and that her life will be lived to the fullest. Cheers!" The mayor raised a glass and drank, and the crowd followed suit. "Now, back to the party everyone!" More cheers went up and the people went back to their talking, playing games, and drinking.

"He wasn't trying to embarrass you," Jace said in her ear. Eva turned toward Jace, and he was smiling down at her. She looked him over. He was wearing well-made shirt and trousers. The clothes contoured to his form where she could take in his well-defined muscles. He had a strong chin and a slight dimple appeared in his cheek when he smiled.

A fire was started a little while ago because night had come. His eyes twinkled blue as he took her in as well. He took a drink from the cup he was holding.

"I got you a present," he told her and proceeded to dig in his pockets. He checked several before coming up empty. "I must have left it in my room."

"You can give it to me later, when I give you your gift."

"You got one for me?"

"Yes, and unlike you I do have it in my pocket. I've just decided that I would rather give it to you when you give me mine." He chuckled at her response.

"It's a deal." Some young men yelled at Jace to come over to them. He looked at her apologetically and started walking toward them. "I'll catch up with you later." She watched him go.

Eva told herself it was fine. He hadn't been here for many years, and he needed to catch up with people. He didn't have to hang around her every second, even though she really wanted him to pay attention to her.

One of the young men she recognized from training, Devon. He showed some promise with a bow. As she looked at the young man, she had a vision.

She saw Devon ask Sonya to go with him. Sonya agreed and they separated from the party. The vision showed Devon asked Sonya something and by the look on her face she said no. Devon wasn't having it and roughly grabbed Sonya.

Eva shivered at what her vision turned into.

Devon forced himself on Sonya. The image skipped in time to the young girl alone in her room, staring blankly at the world, her innocence taken from her. She was riddled with guilt and felt alone in her suffering. The vision shifted again showing Sonya down by the pond, looking at its smooth surface. She pulled out a dagger and plunged it into her chest, not able to bare the reminder of what happened to her.

Eva came back to and noticed that she stood by herself and Devon and the group of men he was with had moved to a different location. Eva was breathing heavily and had to close her eyes to calm herself. She felt a hand shake her arm.

"Come on Eva. We're going close to the fire since that's where all the boys just went to." It was Sonya. Before she could get away, Eva grabbed her sleeve stopping her.

"Sonya, can I ask you something?"

"Sure," she answered with her usual peppy self.

"If Devon asks you to go with him, say no."

"Why would Devon ask me something? Did he say something to you?"

"No. Just, please, for me. If he asks, just say no." Sonya looked over at Devon then back to Eva. It was like she was figuring out a puzzle and a slow smile crept onto her face. Eva didn't know what that was about, but she was relieved by Sonya's answer.

"Sure Eva. I won't get in the way." Before Eva could ask her what she meant, Sonya was now tugging at her to join her at the fire.

Eva hoped that she did the right thing. She only changed something once before and it worked out so she was hoping that this would go the same. She just didn't know what the alternative outcome would be, just so long as it wasn't the outcome she saw.

Chapter 22
Attacked

He couldn't stop looking at her. Jace was constantly searching for Eva. When she came down to the party hours ago in the green dress that she wore, she stood out to him above any other. She was tall but she walked gracefully. No other woman could compare with Eva.

The dress outlined her curves and her hair flowed down her back and looked like silk. He was tempted earlier to just run a few ringlets through his fingers. He absently placed a hand in his pocket where he kept her lock of hair that she gave him before he left for school. He placed it against his palm often, reminding himself of who he was trying to return to.

And that person stood there with a group of women silently listening and sipping on a beverage. He was thinking about how she felt about this whole event. He had to admit that it felt good to be home and hanging with many of the boys that he used to train with. They all were grown now and most of what they talked about was nothing like when they were young.

"So, what do you think my chances are with her?" the blonde-haired boy named Jordie asked at his side.

"With whom?" Jace asked.

"Well duh, Eva of course." Jace probably had a look like he was going to kill Jordie right on the spot for even speaking Eva's name. "I mean, unless she's not available or something," Jordie answered nervously, most likely seeing the look on Jace's face.

"To answer your question," Tad jumped in, "No, there would be no chance with Eva." Tad was almost as tall as Jace with short brown hair. He has a blacksmith's apprentice, so he had a little bit of muscle, unlike Jordie who was about five-foot-ten in height but gangly.

Jace smirked at Tad's response. "Oh, and you think you could have a shot Tad," Jordie laughed. All Tad did was shrug and went back to sipping his drink. "Well, there's always Sasha."

Jace instinctively grabbed Jordie by the scruff of his shirt and hulled him close to his face.

"What about her?" Jace growled into his face.

"Nothing!" Jordie squeaked out.

"You better watch who you're talking with Jordie or you're likely to get punched in the face," Tad mentioned with a smirk on his face watching what unfolded.

Jace lowered Jordie back down and released him. Jordie rolled his shoulders and straightened his shirt front.

"My sisters are off limits," Jace said in a low threatening voice. Jordie throw his hands up in surrender.

"Okay dude. Sorry about that. I just can't help it. Your sisters are very pretty."

Tad was laughing and slapped Jordie on the back, "Seriously man. Just stop talking."

Jordie finally shut his mouth and went back to his drink. At the mention of his sisters, Jace glanced around and found them both. He used to be able to tell them apart, but he'd been gone for so long he was having a hard time identifying them. Sonya, or maybe it was Sasha, was talking with Devon and the other sister was over with two young woman pointing at a boy and then huddling close and giggling.

His gaze went back to the other sister who seemed to be finished up talking and went to join her twin in the group of girls. Both his sisters had moved passed being children. They were four years in age difference from Jace and when he left for school, he remembered them still being cute and innocent.

He could see that they turned quite a few heads now, both taking after their mother with blonde hair and blue eyes and radiant beauty. They were going to break a few hearts. He shook his head at the thought.

That was one thing that Jace didn't want to do. He noticed a few of the young women glanced his direction and when his eye caught them looking, they usually blushed and turned away. Women were so weird. He scanned around to see if he could catch one woman's eyes watching him.

But as he looked over the people twice, he realized that she was gone. He made his way toward the last place she was, which was with the group of young ladies. His sister broke away from the group to trot off toward the drinks and Jace caught up with her.

"Hey sis, have you seen Eva?"

"Um, yeah." He could see that his sister might have partaken in some of the adult beverages.

"You've been drinking, haven't you?"

"Oh Jace, please don't tell mother. I swear I'll do anything, just don't get me in trouble."

"Do you know where Eva went?" His sister rolled her eyes and responded.

"Yeah, she said she was getting tired and headed back toward the house."

"Alone?"

"Yeah? Why, is it that a big problem? She always is alone."

"When you leave this party, take your sister with you. You are not to walk around alone."

"Fine. You won't tell mother on me, will you?" He didn't respond. He wanted to make sure Eva was okay. He started in the direction of the house.

His sister was right, Eva walked by herself all the time. Why was this occasion any different? It wasn't a far walk, but it was not lit and there was just a small, wooded area to go through.

As he walked up the path, he did hear some talking up ahead. He was getting rather close and started to pick up on the conversation.

"There is no need to hurry there. I can make sure you get home safe."

"Release me," that was Eva. Jace picked up his pace.

"You can't deny a man a little taste," the man said sneeringly. Jace heard a grunt as if someone was punched.

"I said no. Leave me alone." Jace was close enough now that he saw the man was bent over and Eva turned to continue toward the house. The man growled and went straight at her. Jace was still too far away.

He watched as Eva was tackled from behind and the man wrenched back her head by her hair. His other hand grabbed the back of her dress and Jace heard the ripping of material. She was pinned under his weight and was struggling to get enough room to move out from under him.

The man came close to her ear and started to say something, but a yell rang out as Jace realized Eva just poked him in the eye as he was covering it, releasing his hold on her hair which then she subsequently head butted him in the nose.

Now with both of his hands covering his face, she was able to buck him off and she scrabbled back to her feet. Jace was almost there.

"You'll get what you deserve bitch," the man growled and went for Eva again. Before he could touch her, he stopped in his tracks grabbing his head and screamed. The man dropped to his knees and then unto his side, curling up into a fetal position.

Jace slowed and walked right up to Eva as the man lay groaning at her feet. He touched her bare shoulder and got an intense feeling of anger. He immediately released her shoulder and quietly said, "Eva."

He noticed her eyes blinked a few times as she turned her head toward him. The man on the ground seemed to have stopped whimpering. Eva looked so vulnerable, her dress barely staying up. He turned his fierce gaze to the man who did this to her.

Jace bent down and hulled him to his feet. It was Devon. He did not expect this of him.

"If I ever see you near Eva or any of my other family members, I will snap your neck in half," he menacingly said into Devon's ear. "Do I make myself clear?"

Devon's blooded face from his broken nose made him look pathetic. Jace pushed him away and he stumbled slightly on his feet.

"Get out of here before I do away with you right now." Devon's eyes widened as he took in the feral look in Jace's eyes. The bastard backed away holding his nose and made his way back down the path. Jace would have to pay a visit to him later.

He turned back toward Eva and their eyes connected. Jace softened his took and immediately came toward her. He gathered her in his arms and crushed her to his chest. He felt them connect and could feel her relief. She still was angry, as she should be. But he needed to be calm for her and not feed into the anger. He could easily do so when it came to Eva.

He pulled his head away to carefully inspect her face. He didn't let her go quite yet.

"You're safe," he breathed out, not realizing he had held it in. She reached up and touched the side of his face. And then she launched herself at him and wrapped her hands around his neck and held on. He held her there making sure he relayed to her that nothing was going to get her.

Jace didn't know how long they stood there but eventually they both pulled back from each other. He smiled down at her and sighed in exhaustion.

"Let's go home," he said softly. She nodded in response. She adjusted her dress and tried to cover as much as she could. He helped by gathering the material up that was ripped in the back and holding it against her. He wrapped his other arm around her shoulders and led her the rest of the way to the house.

They would have to talk eventually about what he saw. She dropped Devon to the ground without touching him. But that was for another time. Right now, his priority was to get her safely inside.

Chapter 23
Misunderstood

He strained against the ropes that bound his hands. It was no use. Number 034 sat in a mountain cave where he was taken after being ambushed on the trail. The people that found him took and blindfolded him, so he didn't know exactly where he was, but he was sure he was somewhere in the mountain range he came upon.

He believed that he was getting close to his destination. Although maybe this was where he needed to be. He thought that he would get a better welcoming, but in these times, I guess that was asking for too much.

Footsteps sounded against the walls and a small light appeared in the passageway across from him. He had lived off and on in total darkness before, so he didn't even realize that there was no light in the cave they had him in.

The person with the light stepped through the entrance and put the torch in a holder on the wall. When his eyes adjusted, there was a woman standing there, draped in a long reddish-brown cloak. Her hair was a very interesting color. It was a deep red, like the color of rubies, but maybe that was just what it looked like because of the low lighting.

More footsteps approached and three others joined the woman. They were all man of varying height. The long-haired woman approached Number 034 and stopped just beyond his reach. Not that he could reach out anyway with his hands tied.

"Please," Number 034 began, "release me. I must be on my way." He had said this before but received no response. The woman looked at him with a smirk. It was like she knew something that he didn't. That was fine. He was sure the information he had was more valuable than what she could ever know.

"Now, why would we do that? Was it not you that came to us?" More riddles? He was beginning to hate talking with people.

"I am only seeking one person. Unless that person is here," he left that hanging in the air. She narrowed her eyes, assessing him.

"Why should we believe you, a Numbered? Do you not serve the tyrant Brosch?" He ground his teeth at the question. Did she not know anything? Before he spoke, the air pulsed around her. Interesting, he wondered what she could possibly be doing. He waited just for a second to see.

"I'm not anything to Brosch." There it was, he felt it. He allowed the feeling to glide over his skin. Did she not know who the Numbered were? He continued with his explanation, "Other than a tool that he uses every once and awhile, a tool he carelessly discarded and is probably now realizing his mistake."

"So, you admit to helping him?" Her eyes narrowed at him. He started to feel now what she was trying to do. He closed his eyes to lock in on the pulse. She was trying to manipulate him in speaking the truth. The woman was a Seeker. Not a common ability, but one that with mastery can be very beneficial in getting information.

Number 034 did not have the ability to stop her prodding, but at least now he knew what she was after. It wasn't like he had any reason to lie to her anyway. He was on an important mission and if telling these people, his own kind, people with the Might, he could have a chance at completing his task.

"Forced to. If I had the choice, I wouldn't." She nodded her head slowly at his response. Her brows scrunched, probably not liking the answer he gave, but it was the truth, just like she was asking for.

"What is your purpose for coming here?"

"As I have said I am only seeking one person. I am only following the information I was given. If that led me here, then this is where I need to be. If I'm not supposed to be here, then let me be on my way to continue my journey."

"And what journey is that?"

"The only important one." He didn't want to go into too much detail. Although she had the Might it didn't mean he would automatically trust her. Her smile became almost predatory. She obviously liked straight forward answers and he was being vague.

He didn't know what she was thinking and maybe she was going to do something, but another person joined in at that moment. She must have been just hiding in the shadows of the doorway for she stepped into the light as if she materialized there. Her hood was up but her face was still peeking out. She was an older woman with snowy-white hair. For a second her eyes seemed to be white, but they were very pale blue.

"You were sent to search for the Child," her wispy voice said. Number 034 nodded his head. She moved closer, the other woman trying to hold her back, but she waved her off and continued forward. She knelt in front of him looking steadily into his eyes. "Where?"

"I was only told to go south." He felt a small sensation crawl up his spin.

"Tell me." That sensation was making him feel compelled to speak, but he didn't know what exactly she wanted to know. "What does the Child look like?"

"I do not know. I was only told I would know the person I seek when I arrive." The old woman stood and turned to the group of people.

"It has begun. The prophesy will happen in our lifetime." She turned back to him her smile soft. "We'll let the Child come to us. We cannot let you leave, but we will make sure you are fed and comfortable."

He was compelled to do as she said, even though in the back of his mind he knew that wasn't what he decided to do. Number 034 would just have to wait. He sure hoped the Child knew to come. The people of this country depended on it.

Chapter 24
Secrets

Kalvin still wasn't feeling well two days after his son's and Eva's coming of age party. If he was honest with himself, he hadn't been feeling well for the last month. He seemed to be steadily getting worse. He had a feeling that this wasn't a normal every day cold.

He was getting tired more often and he had a loss of appetite. He was always a strong leader and hated feeling even a slight bit weak. He had to admit that he did feel weak today.

Kalvin made his way out to the back lawn after looking over some disturbing reports. He received news from Newly that there were several sightings of Chasers close to his stronghold and at Xander Stronghold. There were rumors that one of the Numbered had escaped.

A few Numbered had escaped in the past with the help of Newly and Holds. Both leaders felt that it was their mission to free these people, since most had been taken when they were children. This occurrence was different. Most Numbered that free themselves without help are captured very soon after their attempted escape. The Chasers have not gone beyond Brosch's territory, until now. If the Chasers are still pursuing, then that means this Numbered is a highly prized individual. Brosch would want this person back.

Kalvin took a deep calming breath as he made his way across the lawn. Newly had a few questions and he believed Eva held the answers. Kalvin tried to not bring up such a painful experience to Eva and had been successful at avoiding it. But he realized the importance of finding out what she knew.

He spotted her sitting under the tree near the pond reading a book. She was very structured in her day, reading in the morning then training at the practice field, walking in town and the village, and then more training. Her only changes were in the evening where she alternated from practicing the lyre or flute, needlepoint, or pacing the house property.

Kalvin reached her side and his shadow descended over Eva. She looked up from her book with a raised eyebrow, probably wondering what he wanted.

"Eva, come sit with me." He waved his hand toward some chairs since he knew that it would be impossible for him to get on the ground and back up. She got to her feet and followed him over to the indicated chairs. He sat down with relief. She placed her book on the small table and sat in the chair next to him.

"I hope that you enjoyed yourself the other night. It always surprises me how much all of you have grown," he began. "I know my daughters will soon be of age and I just don't want to think about them leaving the roost."

"I appreciate everything that you have done for me sir. You've treated me like one of your own and I am eternally grateful for that." He smiled at Eva's response. He remembered when she didn't speak at all and now, she spoke so refined and with such knowledge. He always enjoyed talking with her since her ideas had a great influence on what he changed in and around the stronghold.

"Trust me, I'm the one that has been blessed by your presence." Her small smile made his heart warm-up. Like any of his children, all he wanted for her was the best. "Now that you are an adult, there are some things that we need to discuss."

"I understand sir," she nodded.

"Adults sometimes need to discuss difficult topics. And your past Eva, is one of those difficult topics." He saw her brow scrunch and her fingers started to fidget with her skirt. "I have not forced you to answer any questions and I have been patient with you on this. However, I cannot wait any longer. There have been some recent events that require some more detailed explanations that we just don't have. Maybe your experience can be of assistance. You understand what I am asking of you?"

"Yes sir." Her eyes were downcast, but she nodded her head slowly. He leaned forward and rested his elbows on his knees.

"Eva, how long were you in the tower before Holds and Newly found you?"

"I'm not sure. I lost track of time when I was there. It had been a while though."

"Had you ever met Brosch?" Eva's brow scrunched as she was thinking on that question.

"Not at the tower," she answered with a slow head shake.

"Who was at the tower?"

"Usually just the guards. Occasionally the men in red robes would come." She lifted her head and looked off into the distance as if remembering a moment of her past.

"What was their purpose?"

"No one spoke to me," she said still looking lost in her thoughts. "They poked, cut, burned, but I didn't ever get a reason why they did it." She looked down at her hands and just shook her head.

Kalvin didn't know that so much happened to Eva. "Do you know why they kept you there?" Her hands stopped their fidgeting, and she became very still. He could tell that she was nervous about telling him. He had a suspicion as to why Brosch would keep her, but she was missing a critical piece.

"I understand if that information is hard to remember but it might be helpful to our cause. You see, Newly and Holds have been trying their best to free as many children as they can. They are starting to free adults as well, ones that were taken when they were young. They all have a distinct marking on them. Brosch wanted to keep track of them all, so he branded them." To Kalvin it was a barbaric method.

"He placed a number here," he reached over and took Eva's hand. He grazed his thumb on the inside of her right wrist. He felt a slight pulling feeling, but it went away as quickly as he felt it. He wasn't going to be bothered by it. He continued, "Branded into their skin." He looked into her eyes which have grown wide. "But you don't have one."

Kalvin released her hand and sat back in his chair with a sigh. Eva was now rubbing her wrist and her brow was scrunched as if thinking of a problem.

"Eva, I don't want to push the information out of you. When you're ready to talk, I'll be waiting." He stood and steadied himself before making his way back toward the house. "Oh, and Eva," he turned to address her one last time. "If you can also remember what happened to the guards the night you were found, it would ease some of Newly's worries." She nodded her head slowly and then turned to look back off in the distance.

He made his way back to his study, somewhat disappointed that Eva wasn't willing to share everything she could. He had to admit that he did not know how she felt being in that tower dungeon for so long and what happened to her there. He hoped that she would come around and hopefully help in the cause to save the country from tyranny.

Chapter 25
Unravelling

Jace made his way through the house having come from outside. He had just finished some training this morning and was surprised that Eva had not been out in the yard. The tension between them was razor sharp after what happened at the party.

He made sure his message was clear to that bastard Devon the next day. He didn't regret punching the young man in the face and strictly forbidding him to speak of the incident and to stay clear of Eva and his sisters because if he didn't, Jace was going to make sure he did more than just give him a good beating.

Devon kept his word so far, not even telling people how me received the black eye and split lip. Jace didn't know how long it would last but at least he was placid for now. As he made his way past the parlor, his sister came bounding out.

"Hey, Sonya?" he wasn't sure if he had the right name. She stopped and gave him a warm smile.

"Hi Jace. What's up?"

"Have you seen Eva?"

"Wasn't she at the practice field?"

"No."

"Well, that's strange, she's always training in the morning," his sister said as she puckered her lips and tapped her chin with her index finger. Sonya gave it some thought and then shrugged. "I don't know. Maybe she went walking around town or went down to the village. She usually does that after training."

"Alright. I'll look there. Does she normally miss training?" Her sister shook her head making her curls bounce.

"No. She's usually predictable." Jace nodded and was about to go when his sister kept going. "Then again, maybe she wanted to comfort

Devon, you know with him being in the condition he is in." That stopped Jace in his tracks.

"What?" He was unsure why his sister would bring that up.

"Oh, the other night, when Eva told me not to go with Devon, I gathered that it was because she liked him. You wouldn't understand since its girl code."

"You're right I don't understand how you would think she liked Devon from her telling you not to go with him."

"Well duh, why else would she tell me that?" Jace's insides were churning. What Sonya was saying wasn't right. He clearly saw Eva refuse Devon and made sure that he went down to the ground for touching her. But now he was confused.

"I have to find her," he turned on his heel and headed out the door.

"Maybe you should go by Devon's place, she might be there," Sonya called after him. He knew that she wouldn't be there. If she was there, it was to give that bastard a black eye herself.

As he made his way out of the house and down the streets of town, he was thinking too much. Did she like Devon? Of course, she didn't. He needed to stop listening to his sisters. They gossiped and sometimes they were wrong. That activity was going to get them in trouble one of these days.

He didn't realize he was on autopilot until his feet took him out of the stronghold into the surrounding village. When he finally was able to realize where he was, he was walking out toward the lookout post. Why he thought to go there, he didn't know. It was like he was being pulled there by an invisible thread.

He slowed when he neared the post, seeing that there was indeed someone up in it. He wouldn't know until he climbed up there and saw for himself. He very easily scaled the ladder and when his head poked over the ledge of the platform, there she was.

Eva was standing with her arms leaning on the railing looking out to the north. Jace made his way onto the tiny platform and rested against the railing next to her.

Her gaze was looking out, her brow down as if she were frowning. Her ebony hair was braided around the temples and swooped around to join in a thicker braid that ran down her back. She wasn't in the usual garb she wore at trainings, but she was surprisingly in a lovely, blue-colored dress.

"What are you doing?" he asked.

"Waiting."

"For?" She shook her head and looked down. Her hand absently went to the object that he had given her as a gift. He was glad to see that she was wearing the heart-shaped necklace.

"Maybe I miscalculated the time," she mumbled to herself. She seemed to be lost in her own thoughts. "Something could have happened."

"Eva," he touched the back of his fingers to her cheek to get her attention. The familiar feeling sparked, and the contact made her move her head and lock eyes with him. "What are you waiting for? Or who are you waiting for?" She looked back out across the land.

"Obviously someone who isn't coming."

"I'm curious as to how you know someone is coming. Better yet, it reminds me of when I first came back. You were waiting for me."

"I was," she nodded her head without looking over at him.

"I also just heard from Sonya that you told her not to go with Devon. Why did you tell her that?" Eva closed her eyes and sighed. She obviously had things weighing on her mind. Her fingers were fiddling with her necklace.

"She said the reason you told her that was because you liked Devon." That got her attention as she turned to him, and her eyebrow was raised.

"What? I didn't say anything of the sort."

"She said it was like girl code or something. She believes that you were interested in Devon because of what you said."

"I had no such feelings toward Devon. I told her not to go with him and that was it."

"Well, that is not how she heard it." Eva just shook her head in disbelief. She didn't realize though that Jace was sighing in relief on the inside. He was glad to hear that she didn't have any feelings for Devon.

"I know you were the one who gave him those bruises I've heard about."

"And how would you know that?" He hadn't told anyone. She smiled sweetly at him and had a small gleam in her eyes.

"You just confirmed my conclusions." Oh, she was a tricky one.

"Seriously though Eva, I need you to tell me how you seem to know when people are doing things. It makes you vulnerable." She looked down at her hands that she clasped together on the railing.

"I don't know how to explain it."

"You can at least try."

"Fine. But I will not discuss it in the open. You never know who could be listening." Jace glanced around and he seriously did not see a single living thing in the immediate area. He knew that people did not have that good of hearing.

"Eva, there is no one around."

"I just have a lot going on and it would be hard for me to explain right now. I need to think on it. I can talk to you later about it."

"Alright. But you will talk to me about it. Deal?"

"Yes," she sighed. Maybe the two of them could finally put together a piece of the puzzle that was Eva. He was sure that she had some type of ability. Why else would Brosch have kept her in a tower? He wondered if she even knew it of herself.

"Jace," she turned to him and laid her hand on his arm. "Have you talked with your father recently?"

"Yeah. I just saw him this morning at breakfast, and we talked about the livestock."

"No, I meant has he talked about how he has been feeling."

"Um, no, why would he? He's fine. Right?" Eva looked up into his eyes. As he gazed into those hazel depths, he realized that Eva knew something that he didn't. "Tell me." Eva blinked a few times. A small smile touched the corner of her mouth but then her face became sad. There was something on her mind.

"Your father is sick."

"What, you mean like a cold? Those go away."

"It isn't a cold."

"The flu can stay for a while, but that eventually goes away as well."

"It's not that."

"Then what is it?"

"Your father came and spoke to me today about my time in the tower. I do feel sorry for not answering all your father's questions, but I was afraid that he would see me as a different person once he heard it."

"He wouldn't treat or see you any differently. I wouldn't. What was done was done. It's not like you can change the past." If only he could, then Eva could never have dealt with what she endured at the tower.

"Well, he was telling me about some of these people that were also rescued from Brosch. They all were branded."

"What, you mean like cattle?" She nodded her head in response. "That's not right."

"Anyway," Eva continued, "Your father was showing me where they were branded and when he held my hand, I connected with him."

"Wait, you had the connection that we usually have, but with my dad?"

"No, well, I did have a connection, but I believe it was only one-sided. I felt his pain Jace. It bled through the connection. He's not well." He thought he was the only one that could connect with Eva in that way. Now it looks like she might be able to connect with others. She was probably going to try to avoid touching as much as possible now.

"He'll get better," he assured her. All she did was slowly shake her head back and forth. Her eyes began to moist, but he could see that she held back the tears.

"It's an illness that he will not be able to recover from." He gathered her up into his arms and she didn't stop him. She clung to him as he stroked her back. "Will you talk with him about it?"

"Of course, I will. If you promise to come talk to me about the other stuff that's going on." He felt her nod her head in agreement against his shoulder. He pulled her back and lifted her chin, so their eyes met. "I don't think your person is coming." She turned and looked out over the land to the north and sighed.

"I think you're right."

"Let me walk you back to the house."

"Okay, I guess so."

"Hey, I know what will keep your mind busy. Why don't you come and spar a little with me at the practice field?"

"I'd like that," she sniffled.

They made their way down the ladder and headed back toward the stronghold. Jace knew there was a lot going on inside Eva's head. He wasn't expecting his father being unwell. He'll just have to confirm it, to ease both their minds.

Chapter 26
Not Good

He coughed into his handkerchief as he settled into his chair behind his desk. Kalvin looked in his palm and sighed. The red splotches could not be good. What was he going to do? He loved his family, but he didn't want them to worry.

He lifted some reports that he hadn't gotten to earlier and began reading them. Two swift knocks sounded against the door. He glanced up to see his son standing in the entrance.

"Hey dad, can I speak with you?"

"Sure, you can. Come in." Kalvin wasn't in the mood to read reports anyways. He put his piece of paper down and watched his son enter and sit in the chair just opposite him. Jace ran his fingers through his hair, and he looked to be uneasy. "Is something wrong?"

"What? Oh, no, not with me," his son shook his head. He ran his hand back through his hair again, making the ends go all which way.

"You know you can tell me anything son." Jace let out a pent-up breath and finally looked his father in the eye.

"Are you sick?" Kalvin didn't expect that question. His eyes widened, he recovered as quickly as he could, but not before Jace recognized it. "You are. Tell me why you've kept it to yourself."

"Don't get the wrong idea. Do you think I didn't want to tell all of you?" Kalvin sighed and ran his hand down his face.

"Maybe a Healer can help."

"A Healer? And where am I going to find one? You know that they are few and far between like any other person with the Might."

"We need to try something." He could understand his son's persistence. The only issue was that Kalvin knew the extent the Healers could go, and he was pretty sure that he was beyond their help.

"The truth is I've been in a bad way for a while now. There's nothing that can be done at this point." His son angrily got to his feet and stormed over to the window. Kalvin couldn't fathom what his son must be feeling. His son had spent most of his life apart from Kalvin, first because of the Great War and then because of Brosch and that stupid boy's school.

"Son, I've lived a full life. I'll admit that I'm not ready to die, but what can I do?"

"I'm just," Jace sighed, his shoulders noticeably slouching. "I'm just not ready to say goodbye." Kalvin chuckled slightly.

"I'm not dying tomorrow. Come here, sit." His son came away from the window and settled himself back into the chair he had occupied just a moment ago.

"Promise me something father. Promise me you will tell the rest of the family about it. Don't keep them out of the loop."

"I promise."

"Soon dad, like tonight if possible."

"Alright son. I will."

"Good." They both sat there in silence for a moment, letting everything sink in. If Kalvin were honest with himself, it felt like a weight was lifted off his chest. It was killing him not being able to speak about it.

"Well, I'll get going," Jace finally said and stood. He started toward the door and before leaving he turned to say over his shoulder, "I love you dad."

"I love you too, Jace." His son nodded his head and continued walking out. Kalvin wished he could change his circumstances, spend more time with his boy.

He slowly breathed in and out, not knowing what time he had left with his family, but the time he did have, he'd make sure they knew that he loved them.

Chapter 27
The Truth

He stood by the window looking out into the darkness. Jace's thoughts were churning a mile a minute. Eva had been right. His father was not well. He was sick enough that he believed that he couldn't be cured, that nothing would help him. There must be a way. He couldn't lose his father.

He looked up at the stars, silently hating how bright and happy they looked, because he didn't feel anything like that.

A small squeak and shuffling of feet from behind him could only mean one thing. Eva was here. The shuffling feet stopped next to him and when he glanced over, there she was. The light from the night sky illuminated her face, outlining her eyes. In the white nightgown she looked like an ethereal being sent from the afterlife.

He went to look back out into the night. Eva let him, joining him without interrupting his thoughts. Her presence gave him comfort. She didn't even have to say anything. It was one quality that others might not like, being that she just walks up and does not say anything.

Jace wasn't aware that he had no other lights going besides the soft glow of the fireplace. Learning about his father's illness gave him chills and he didn't know any other way to feel better. He turned away from the window and sat on the edge of the bed.

Eva stood there with her back to him, but he knew that she was waiting for his input on the information she told him earlier that day.

"So, I spoke with my father," Jace began. "You were right." He hung his head and shook it slightly still not believing it. He watched as she slowly turned around and faced him. It was interesting that the light of the fire changed how she looked. He now imagined her as a goddess that could yield fire. Oh, if only that was an ability.

He looked down at his hands, picking under his nail at invisible dirt. Her shadow came closer, and her feet came into his vision just in front of him, mere inches away. Huh, he never noticed that she was shoeless before. He looked up and saw that she was very concerned. Why wouldn't she be? His father took her in. It made sense that she was worried about him as well.

Eva came and sat next to him. She took his hand and threaded their fingers. It was a very intimate contact, but because of their connection, he was able to feel her giving him warmth and comfort. She rested her head on his shoulder. He felt comforted by the action and feeling the empathy from their connection was interesting. It was a deep feeling, it was there only briefly though, not long enough for him to try and unravel it.

"I don't want him to die," she said. He let go of her hand and brought his arm around her shoulders and pulled her to him.

"I don't either. He just seems to think there isn't something that can be done. He won't even try a Healer."

"A Healer?" she asked, looking up at him with the scrunched brow of hers. Her thinking look.

"Yeah, someone with ability to heal. It would have to be someone with the Might. That's where the problem is. Finding someone like that."

"What do Healers normally do?"

"I don't know specifically, but they definitely can heal up some cuts and bruises, mend broken bones in a fraction of the time, and I think ease pain."

"You've seen this?"

"No, just have heard stories. It was commonplace before the Great War that a mayor would try to at least have one Healer within his stronghold. People with the Might were seen as exceptional people and their ability was a gift to this land. Brosch views them as a disease. He's the one that is a disease on this land. He hasn't done anything that has made this country prosperous. It won't be long until we get overrun by another country, and since ours is so broken, there would be no way to stop such an attack."

"You've learned about the Might at school?" He snorted at the question.

"No. That was one topic they tried to avoid often. It did come up, but it wasn't enough detail to really know the different abilities."

"Where did you learn it?"

"From my Nanna," he smiled at the memory of his beloved grandmother. "She would go on and on about it. I realize now that I am older, I should have tried to pay more attention to her ramblings. But I was kid. It's not like I could understand it at the time."

"Did she ever talk about auras?"

"A little bit," he looked at Eva, her head was down, and she was fiddling with her necklace. "How did you hear about auras?"

"Oh, I read it in a book I found in the library."

"Really? I don't remember a book like that being in the library."

"It was on the very top shelf behind some other books. I just happened to see it when I was selecting the book in front of it. I put it back."

"Hey, you didn't do anything wrong. Did you learn anything valuable?" She nodded her head and a small smile appeared on her lips. "Name one thing that you learned."

"Well, I learned that we each have an aura, and each color means different areas that we would be good at. It is only when a person uses that ability at a massive energy level that the person would be considered someone with Might." That was interesting. Jace wanted to see this book for himself, just so he can catch up on what he remembered as a boy from his Nanna.

"I remember Nanna mentioning something about auras to me. This one time she was just sitting there preparing a meal and suddenly turned to me, eyes shining with this huge smile on her face. She said, 'Jace. One day you will meet your aura's match. Nothing will be able to stop you once your auras merge.' Yeah," he chuckled to himself. "She was a nutter, but I loved her."

"How do auras merge?" Her eyes were large and sparkling at the idea.

"I have no idea. I didn't think to ask her at the time what she meant. Trust me she said a lot of stuff that didn't make sense." She nodded her head slowly. He touched her cheek softly, now loving the familiar pull from the connection. "Now, enough about auras and stuff, you have some things that need to be explained."

"I know," Eva sighed. Jace stood and went over to his washstand. A pitcher of water sat ready for use. He took the pitcher and an empty glass and began pouring himself a drink. "Where do I start?" He turned back to her and brought the glass to his lips to take a drink. He watched as she got up and moved to the window again, leaning against the frame with her arms crossed.

"How about you talk about why you think my father would change his opinion of you," he suggested. He drained his glass and refilled it. He stepped up next to her, waiting for her to speak.

"It's not because I don't appreciate life," she said softly. He could see how her eyes had that far off look to them. He lightly touched her shoulder and held the glass of water out to her. "Thanks." She took the glass in her two hands and took a small drink.

"What would make us think otherwise?"

"Because of why I was placed in the tower in the first place," she went back to looking out into the night, afraid to look at him. He brushed one of her loose strands behind her ear. With the soft brush he tried to send her comforting thoughts. She sighed and placed the glass of water on the window ledge.

"At first, I didn't know why they held me. I asked until I realized they would never give me the answer. It's like my brain shut out what I did. But, now that I'm older, snippets come to the forefront of my mind. Images of the worst night of my life." She closed her eyes and took a deep shuttering breath. Jace placed a hand on her back and rubbed up and down slowly.

"And what would cause grown men to put a small child into a dungeon? How old were you anyway when they captured you?"

"Not very old. I was in that tower a long time before Gene and Penn came."

"Okay, so let's say you were three. What could a three-year-old do that would scare everyone to lock her away?" Eva turned toward him and looked into his eyes. He could have sworn he saw them flicker totally black for a second, but he must have been imagining it because when he looked, they were the hazel color he was used to seeing.

"Would you believe me if I said that I made sure I wasn't slaughtered like my family was? That by instinct I let myself," she paused looking down and shaking her head. She obviously was having trouble saying it.

He then remembered how she dropped Devon to the ground, grabbing his head in pain. He grabbed her shoulders and took his own calming breath. "Are you trying to say that you took them down like you did Devon?" She looked up at him with a pleading look.

"Worse."

"You killed them," he dropped his hands back to his side.

"Does that make me a bad person?"

"You would have died," he said matter-of-factly, trying to come to terms with what she was saying. "They would have killed an innocent child." He shouldn't say that he was glad that she did it.

"I honestly didn't know what I did. I just made it so they wouldn't hurt me, ever." She brought her arms around herself.

"Hey," he noticed that she was backing away and had a sense that she was not sure how he felt about her. She didn't protest as he brought his arms around her. "You are still Eva. You had your reasons for what you did." He tilted her chin so their eyes would meet. "That doesn't change who you are, just who you became. You've trained and worked hard. You're able to take an opponent down with a burst of air! You couldn't do that when you were three. You had no other option against men four times the size you were. I would never have met you if you didn't kill those men and were taken to the tower. I wish I could take those bad memories from you, but if events didn't happen as they did you would have never come to stay with my family. I'm sorry your family was killed."

"I don't let myself even glimpse in the past to remember what they looked like; I get too sad." A single tear rolled down her cheek. He brushed it away with his thumb. "Is it the same with the other children that were taken by Brosch? Did he have their families killed?"

"I'm not sure. He'll threaten and will act on it if he encounters resistance, but most just give in, hoping that one day they will see their child again." She nodded her head slowly.

"He takes children, innocent lives."

"Yeah. He wants to change the next generation's thinking. Children are the future." They stood there looking at each other for a moment. Before he could say anything more about what he experienced at school, Eva's eyes turned pure white.

"The Child of the Mighty will bring light to the darkness," Eva said in a very emotionless monotone voice. Her eyes flickered and blinked and when they did, they were no longer white.

Oh Fates, she was a Seer! It all made sense to Jace now. She must have seen things in the future, like him coming home. His Nanna was a Seer and had seen her go into a trance several times. Except, he didn't remember his Nanna speaking aloud in a trance. Was that different?

"What is it?" Eva interrupted his thoughts.

"Nothing. Just tired." He wondered if she even knew what she was. "We can discuss the other stuff later." He released her and smiled kindly at her, to not make it look like he just wanted a little space to think.

"Oh, okay." She walked toward the door, obviously unaware of what she had said when in a trance. Did she even know that she was in one? She turned back when she reached the door and as she shut it, she said, "Good night."

"Good night, Eva." The door clicked shut and Jace was left standing there looking at the closed door. What Eva could do changed everything. And what he remembered from his Nanna, talking aloud meant something. Maybe some sleep will help him remember.

Chapter 28
Seers and Prophesies

"Father, may I come in?" Jace had poked his head into the library. Kalvin was just reading about the history of Hockland, familiarizing himself with the events of the past leading up to the Great War. It had been hard that morning announcing at breakfast of his situation. No one responded like he expected. His wife rose slowly from her seat and walked out without a word. He still needed to go find her and probably brace for the backlash that he knew was coming.

His daughters didn't know what to say, after seeing their mother leave, they were unsure of what to do. They sat with their heads down, silently picking at their meal. Jace and Eva seemed to not react at all. That just meant they already knew, which he'd suspected that Eva would have learned about it from Jace. They seemed to talk about everything together. If one knew, the other knew too.

He set his book down on the small table next to him. "Of course, son." Jace entered and sat across from him on the small sofa. His arms rested on his knees and his hands were clasped together. He knew that pose. Jace had something on his mind. "What's it about? Not any bad news, I hope. This family probably can't take any more bad news today."

"No, it's not bad news." His son sat back into the sofa and expelled air through slightly puffed cheeks. "I'm just wondering about something I heard."

"And what did you hear?"

"Well, I think it was a prophesy. I didn't know if this one was already said. If I remember correctly, the more times it is said, the better probability that the prophesy will come true?"

"You are correct. A prophesy is only viable in the number of times that it has been foretold. Can I ask what you heard?"

"Well, it was about a Child of the Mighty. I was wondering if you had heard about a prophesy referencing a child?"

"Where'd you hear about this?" His son shifted in his seat. He was uncomfortable with the question.

"Say I heard it when I was traveling, a passing rumor if you will."

"What exactly was the prophesy?"

"It was about this child bringing light to the darkness. Whatever that could mean." Jace shrugged trying to play it off that he wasn't exactly sure. Kalvin suspected that he knew more than he was saying but he wasn't going to push his son on that. "I didn't know if you had heard something, you know, since you've been around longer than I have."

Without saying anything, Kalvin rose from his seat and went up to the bookcase. He moved a few books aside on the top shelf and he reached in and found what he was looking for. He brought the item over to Jace and held it out to him. His son took it with a raised eyebrow. "What is this?" his son asked.

"Open it," Kalvin instructed and made his way back to his seat. His son carefully opened it and his eyes glanced at the words written on the first page. His eyes grew large, and he glanced up to his father.

"Is this, Nanna's?"

"Yes." Kalvin knew what it said on the first page. In perfect penmanship it read 'The Journal of Bea Jebrow.' His son stared down at the journal probably in disbelief. "You think my mother could remember everything she said over the years? Most of it is about her life and what she knew about the Might. It was her understanding of the world." His son began flipping through the pages, briefly glancing at the finer details.

"How long has it been here?"

"My mother thought she had the perfect hiding spot, except my father and I knew exactly where it was. She left it here son. She didn't take it with her when you all went into hiding."

"Why am I looking at it now?"

"Here, let me see it," Kalvin held out his hand to take the journal from him. Jace handed it over. Kalvin quickly flipped to the information he knew was in there. He could have told his son, since he was there when it happened, but he wanted his son to read it for himself, from his grandmother's own hand. "Read this," he held the journal opened toward his son.

Jace took it and began reading what was on the page. His son's expression changed from curiosity to bewilderment to confusion. "This doesn't make any sense. What am I reading?"

"It was a prophesy your grandmother had on that day. That was the only time she ever had one to my knowledge. It was so profound and slightly disturbing all at the same time."

"But the date it happened, its," his son just shook his head not wanting to believe.

"Yes, I know. It probably raises a lot more questions than it answers. Trust me, it caused me much grief when I let your grandmother shepherd you away."

"But mother came, and she had Sasha and Sonya."

"I didn't know your mother was pregnant. I was surprised, and relieved that they were safe as well. But your grandmother only wanted to take you. Your mother pleaded to go with you. She didn't want to be separated from her only child at the time."

Jace closed the journal and sat there thinking. He eventually drew his hand down his face and shook his head trying to jog some sense into it. He stood and went over to the fireplace, staring into the small flames that rose from the logs. "She died believing in that prophesy."

"She writes more about it and gives her reasons. I'll let you keep the journal so you can learn for yourself. I've no use for it."

"You realize there is one thing missing that this prophesy describes?"

"Yes," Kalvin sighed. "I even tried to bring it up, but she insisted that she was right. Trust me I thought about it a lot, especially when you were in hiding." Jace came back and sank back down in the sofa. The journal closed in his hand.

"Have you heard other Seers say this prophesy?"

"Exactly? No. But the ones I have heard did involve a child and something or other to do with light and dark."

"Where can I find these records?"

"Not everyone is as meticulous as your grandmother was. I always had my ear open and like you said, you believe it was a rumor."

"Do you believe it a rumor?"

"That," he pointed to the journal, "was the first known mention of the Child. You know how old it is and it was before the Great War. I've only heard just a few after the war was over. It has only picked up in the last few years, which leads me to believe that the prophesy will take place, soon."

"Who would know more about it? I would need to talk with a Seer, right?"

"The only one I can think of is with the underground. I think she is with a group that calls themselves Rens."

"Where do I find these Rens?"

"Newly will know."

"Why him?"

"Newly has made it his mission to save people from Brosch's clutches. You can bet that he saves people with the Might. Where do you think the safest place for them to be once rescued?"

"In the underground."

"Precisely."

"Are they close by?"

"That is a question you would need to ask Newly. These people only trust a few. I'm not part of their few."

"So, it sounds like if I want answers, I need to see Newly?" Kalvin responded by nodding slowly to his son. "You'll be alright with me leaving?"

"How else will you find the answers? Don't you think I might want to know too? Get some closure? You'll be doing this for your mother and I as well." Jace stood from the couch. He looked down at the journal in his hand and brought it up to the jacket he was wearing and placed it in his inside breast pocket.

"So, I should go talk with her?"

"Yes. I need to talk with her as well." Kalvin rose from his seat and took a moment to stretch out his limbs. "I don't think she liked what I told her this morning. Let me butter her up first before you say what you need to say."

"Great, she's going to hate me," his son threw his hands in the air. He clapped his son on his back and chuckled.

"You know your mother so well. Come, let's walk out there together. I'm sure she's in her favorite spot outside."

Kalvin walked out to face his wife with his son beside him. He knew that Jace needed to go on this mission. After nineteen years, maybe they could finally understand his mother's prophesy. Or maybe it would cause the rest of the country to finally know who the Child really was.

Chapter 29
Not so Upset

"When are you leaving?" Lorraine asked her son. They just finished a discussion about some prophesy or other. She had to deal with all that craziness with her mother-in-law and she thought she was done with it. The fact that this one had upset her so long ago and that it still held the same uneasy feeling was enough to understand what her son was going through. Wouldn't it be better to finally find out who this was about instead of taking her mother-in-law's word about it?

"Probably within the week," he answered. She nodded her head. She wasn't thrilled about the idea but what could she do?

"Well, you're a grown man now, I can't stop you."

"Really, you're not mad?"

"Mad? Why would I be mad? Yes, it does seem a little soon after your return. Young people are always on the move. No, I would be mad if you left without telling me." She turned and glared at her husband.

Learning about his illness this morning hadn't surprised her, just that it was more severe than she thought. She was his wife, and she could tell that he was not well, but she wanted him to be honest and tell her. The fact that he didn't tell her up front was what she was angry with him about.

"Lori…" Kalvin implored.

"Don't you Lori me," she snapped. She immediately turned back to her son and gave him a warm smile. "I knew one day that it would come back up. And honestly, it would be one less thing I would worry about."

"I won't be gone long."

"I know dear. You'll be gone as long as you need to be."

"I can't believe that you are okay with this mother."

"Well, it's obvious that your father is okay with it, since I assume you did talk to him about it first?"

"I did."

"Then if he's okay with it, I'm okay with it. Although, I'm thinking there might be a certain someone that might not like that idea," she looked off behind him toward the pond and inclined her head at the woman standing there. Her son turned and visibly tensed. He turned back to her and gave her a shaky smile. "Go on. It's better to do it now." She waved her son away.

He blew some pent-up air from his lungs and got up and walked toward Eva. Lorraine had been paying attention this last month. It was because of Jace that Eva was able to feel comfortable when she first arrived to even talk to anyone and she was by his side every minute of every day. When he was away at school, Eva didn't have any interest in what her daughters were doing and rarely spoke with them.

Now that Jace was back, she noticed a distinct look between her son and Eva. When they were together, it was like the rest of the world around them didn't matter. Granted, Lorraine never caught the two of them holding hands or anything, but it was evident to her that they were very much into each other.

"And why would Eva care?" Kalvin asked sweetly next to her. Ah, yes, her husband. She should be angry with him, but when she turned her head to look at him, her breath caught at his handsomeness. He always had her heart fluttering with that crooked smile and deep blue eyes. She liked his look of strength and always marveled at his physique. It was clear that she couldn't stay mad at him forever. She sighed and turned back to look across the lawn at her son with Eva.

"Kalvin, you do realize that they like each other?"

"What? I did not know this."

"What do you mean?" she turned toward him with a raised eyebrow. "Have you not noticed how much time they spend together? Look at them," she pointed their way. "How can you not see that?" They were sitting too far away to hear the exact words they exchanged but Lorraine could see Eva's expression change quickly.

"I don't see it."

"If Eva didn't like Jace than she wouldn't be getting as mad as she is."

"So?" She scuffed at her husband's question.

"Really, you should know all about your love getting angry with you by now. And that's exactly what is happening right now with them." Kalvin reached over and threaded his fingers with hers. He lifted her hand and kissed the back of it. His gazed up and caught her looking at him.

"Are you angry Lori? Did I truly mess up this time?" Again, she couldn't be mad at him for long. She raised her free hand and stroked down his cheek.

"No, I'm not angry. I was upset that you didn't tell me right away."

"I didn't want to worry you."

"So, you let me worry without knowing what I was so worried about?"

"I love you too much to see you suffer because of me."

"I love you Kal, but you can't hide things from me. At least I can try to cope with it now that I know what is going on. Before, I didn't know what I needed to cope with." She turned back toward the young couple. Now Eva was very animated, and both seemed to be talking with their hands.

They sat in a comfortable silence watching the two young ones interact, even though it was impossible to hear exactly what they were talking about. After a short time, they witnessed something that shocked everyone. Eva slapped Jace.

Eva even looked at her hand, wondering where it came from. Before Jace could do anything, Eva stormed away. Once Jace recovered from the blow, he ran after her calling her name and asking her to wait.

"Wow. I didn't know Eva had it in her. I mean, I know she's tough and I've seen some pretty good moves on the practice field, but I have never seen her strike anyone like that." Her husband's eyes were wide following the two's retreat into the house.

"Young love can have so many troubles. Remember ours?" Kalvin turned his gaze at her and smiled that lopsided grin of his.

"And which time would that be Lori?" She swatted him playfully on the arm and he chuckled.

"Honestly, I lost count the many times I slapped you."

"I just remember that I wanted you to be mine forever. When I started courting you, for some reason you thought there were others that I'd be seeing, and you would get so jealous over nothing. I think I was slapped the most times because women were looking at me."

"I did not."

"You know, to this day I have no idea who I was attracting, because the only woman I wanted was you Lori," his eyes sparkled with heat. That look still made her blush.

"Let's just forget that I would do anything harmful to your handsome features."

"Right. Well, I better head back in. Would you like to join me sweetheart?"

"Oh, I guess I can. It would be a good time to discuss what you announced earlier today. I think I can compose myself enough to listen to it without possibly slapping you," she gave him a warm smile.

Kalvin stood and offered his arm to her. She stood and slid her arm through his and they lazily walked toward the house. She hoped that she could try and do something for her husband. Even beyond his simple expression she could see pain lines around his eyes. The talk wasn't going to be pleasant, but at least it would ease some worry. She knew though that just talking about it didn't make the problem go away.

Chapter 30
Healer

She looked out her bedroom window with her arms crossed in front of her. The fading light stained the sky orange and pink. Eva stood there thinking about the conversation she had with Jace several days ago. He was vague with specifics. When Eva said that she would go with him, he stated that she wasn't going, but was unwilling to say why.

Well, she wasn't very forthcoming on why she wanted to journey with him. At first it was because she didn't want to be away from him again, but that was absurd. That feeling she was unused to and was unable to place it. The main reason was the vision she had just after she stormed off.

The vision showed the red-haired man from before, but instead of him traveling he was tied up. She didn't feel any immediate danger to his safety in the vision, but she did feel a sense of urgency. He had been waylaid and now if they were to meet, she would have to go to him.

Eva began forming a plan. She was going to go on this journey, but without Jace knowing it. She planned on following him at a distance. She had already snuck some food and other little things needed for the trip. He was planning on leaving mid-day tomorrow. She had been avoiding him since their little disagreement. She was also terribly embarrassed by her actions. She knew that she would just complicate things if she let any of her plans slip out when she was speaking with him.

There was one thing though that settled heavy in the back of her mind. It was the mayor's condition. She'd been thinking about what to do to help him ever since she learned about his illness. The last few nights on her walks through the halls, she heard his terrible coughing.

As the sun dipped behind the horizon and the stars came twinkling into existence in the dark sky, she knew the house would be quiet and she could now leave her room and roam as she pleased.

She had become very good with stealth, having much practice over these last six years. She knew every nook and cranny, all the hidden servant stairs and who was where. She made her way out of her room and down the hall. She passed the twins' room and then Jace's. She scowled slightly at the door still seething about their last conversation. That wasn't her destination tonight.

She continued forward until she reached the door on the opposite side of the hall. This was the master suite. A door further down was the mistress suite but most of the time Lady Jebrow was with her husband.

Eva pressed her ear against the door to determine if everything was normal. She heard a faint raspy breathing, but she did not hear any talking. She also could see that the fireplace was lit because there was flickering light coming from the bottom of the door. It was faint, so there was not a large roaring fire.

She reached out and slightly pressed down on the door handle's mechanism. A soft click responded indicating that it could now be opened. With much control she swung the door inward while gently lifting off the handle. Thank goodness this door didn't squeak like Jace's. She slipped inside and just as carefully closed the door until there was just a slight opening remaining.

As she looked back into the room, her gaze landed at a slumped form in a chair next to the bed. It was Lady Jebrow. She must have fallen asleep while attending to him. Eva quietly made her way to the side of the bed Lady Jebrow was not on and stood. The raspy breathing she heard was coming from the mayor.

It pained her to see him like this. He had been so kind, taking her in when she had no one else. Even though she buried her past and refused to remember, she did have a feeling that she had no other family. The Jebrows were her family now and she would do anything to help the people she had grown to love.

He was too far on the other side for Eva to see him clearly, so she made her way over to the other side of the bed, careful of not disturbing Lady Jebrow. She didn't tell Jace, but she was sure that she had some healing ability. She wasn't entirely sure, but there were several cuts and scrapes that she took care of herself. Oh, and the burns.

She shook her head to clear the memory of searing skin. It was not a smell one can forget. She was here to do a job.

Eva placed her hand on top of his. She didn't feel a connection, not like when he touched her hand last time. She wondered if the connection was only possible when a person was awake. Jace was the only other person she felt that connection with and they usually were awake, so maybe.

The mayor didn't seem to notice her hand, so she continued. She placed her other hand lightly on his forehead, just a light touch. She waited a second, he continued to breathe the same, in that painfully sounding rasp.

Eva closed her eyes and concentrated. She tried to recall the feeling the last time she had healed a small cut on her leg. She was in the practice yard training with a wooden dummy and ended up splintering the thing into small pieces with her force ability. A small shard lodged in her leg and when she removed it, a trickle of blood formed on her leg.

She felt that familiar tingle inside her chest as she thought about removing the pain and stitching the cut up. She pushed that tingle out to travel along her arms to where the mayor lay. She let the invisible thread search for the pain. He had to have pain even though she could not see it on the surface.

It only took a few seconds, and she touched the pain. It was a large feeling that snaked throughout his body. It wasn't concentrated to one area. As she let her thread feel out it became apparent that the mayor was in worse condition than anyone realized. She had never dealt with this much pain before and was unsure if she would be able to take it away.

She had to try, didn't she? Without her, would there be anyone else that could help? Just before she tried to pull the pain, a blinding light filled the darkness behind her eye lids.

As she looked down, the mayor was gone, and she seemed to be standing in front of a clear bench. Eva looked around but she wasn't sure if this was a vision or if she just transported to a different place since it felt tangibly real.

A figure slowly materialized and walked toward her. This was different than a vision. The figure had a flowing white robe and golden hair adorned his head. As he came closer, she tried to detect an aura, but she failed to see one, just like Jace.

The man stopped in front of her and smiled warmly at her.

"Now, what is the reason you summoned me?" he asked. She turned her head to the sides and saw that he must have been talking to her since she was the only one in this white world along with the man who was in front of her.

"I summoned you?"

"Of course, you did." He moved to her side and took a seat on the clear bench. He patted the bench beside him. "Have a seat." She wasn't sure, but she lowered slowly next to him.

His eyes twinkled like diamonds, never staying on a particular color. She'd never seen that before.

"Let's get down to business, shall we?" He took out a small bit of paper from a pocket in his robe and unfurled it. "Name?"

"Um…" He quirked his eyebrow and waited. "Eva."

"Alright then, let me check here." He glanced over the paper in his hand, checking the back as well. "Strange, you are not on my list." Okay. She had no idea what was going on and now she was curious why he just has a list of names in his pocket.

"List?" He waved his hand in the air and pocketed the list.

"Not important." He turned slightly toward her, and his twinkling eyes locked with hers. He continued, "You have a question that needs to be answered."

"What is this place?"

"That wasn't your question, but I will answer all the same. Currently you are at the Station. It's just a meeting place for Sparks. I am guessing this is your first time here." Eva nodded her head, now even more confused. The Station? Sparks?

What was this man talking about? He continued, "In time, you will come to understand, but you need some assistance. That is why you are here."

"How can you help me?"

"I hold the answer to your question."

"I don't remember asking a question."

"Ah, yes. You are uncertain about something though. You still want to continue, even though you do not know what will happen. Wouldn't you want to know what would happen?" The man must have been talking about the mayor. She was just about to take his pain, but the amount of pain was more than she had dealt with before and she was unsure of the outcome.

"He has so much of it. And I don't know what will happen. Can I cure him?" she pleaded with her eyes that she could heal him. The white-robed man's face saddened but his eyes remained caring. Just by his look Eva knew the answer.

"Would you sacrifice your life for his?" She didn't expect that question. He must have seen her questioning look because he continued. "An illness that is meant to kill will do its job, no matter who it is." She thought about his response but did not understand it.

"So, what are you saying?"

"You can take that illness from him, but where does it go? It must go somewhere, doesn't it?"

"You mean, I would get it, since I am taking it?"

"Correct." Oh my. He was saying that if she took the mayor's illness from him, that it would just transfer to her and then she would die. Wow, that was crazy.

She thought about the mayor, and she wanted to do anything to help him since he took her in, but was she willing to sacrifice her life for him? What would he want? Would he want her to sacrifice her life to save him? No, he wouldn't want her to do that. He would lay down his life for his kids, her included. He knew his time was ending and he accepted it.

"Can't I do anything?" she asked.

"What do you think?"

"I can still take the pain away, can't I? He doesn't need to suffer."

"Are you willing to feel that pain yourself?" She realized what he was saying. She would take his pain, but it had to go somewhere just like if she took the illness. She would experience his pain for him.

"Would it be too much for me to endure?"

"Your strength should hold, but if you feel you need more to assist you, you always have your other half." Her what? *"Now I must leave you so you can continue your work."* He rose from the bench and started to walk away.

"But I have other questions."

"Which can be answered at another time," he said over his shoulder.

"I don't even know who you are. How can I call on you again if I do not know your name?"

"Your Spark calls for you, Eva." He slowly disappeared and the light faded.

Eva blinked her eyes and looked around her. She was back in the mayor's chambers and Lady Jebrow was still sleeping in her chair. Her hands were still on the mayor's hand and forehead. She didn't know what she just experienced. Did she just make that up? Whatever it was, she would figure it out later. She knew what she had to do.

She took a deep breath, felt along the thread, and pulled.

Chapter 31
Eventful Night

A loud noise jarred Jace from his sleep. He rubbed his eyes and sat up slightly to look around. His gaze swept the room and landed on a figure standing in the doorway of his bedroom.

"Eva?" he groggily asked. The figure did not move, but he was certain it was her. He turned to the bedside table and lit a candle. As soon as the light flared to life, he let his eyes adjust and take in the room around him. Eva was standing in the doorway.

He yawned and swung his legs to the edge of the bed. "I'm surprised to see you," he said. After their last discussion, she seemed very angry with him. He tried to talk with her the last several days, but she seemed to be avoiding him. She obviously was still not happy with him. Well, he could understand that, but if he told her why he was doing it then what would she think of him?

He thought she was a Seer. Did she even know she was one? They weren't common. If he guessed that she had the Might before, this was a sign that she did have it. Seers had an ability. That ability was what labeled them as a person with Might. A Seer was a person with Might that had visions of future events and can prophesize. Visions were more common in Seers than prophesies. He did want to ask her if she had visions. He was a little suspicious with certain things she did, like warning his sister about Devon and when she had been to the lookout post to wait for people, including waiting for him.

Eva stepped into the room and then collapsed to the floor. Jace sprung from the bed and moved quickly toward her. She was lying on her side breathing in shallow quick breaths. It sounded like she was hyper-ventilating.

"Eva!" he turned her slightly, so she was lying on her back. He took her shoulders and slightly shook her. "Eva!" She was non-responsive. Her eyes were closed but he could see erratic movement behind them. Her brow was scrunched like she was in immense pain. He was at a loss of what to do.

He had to connect with her. That was the only way he could feel what she was feeling. He lightly touched her cheek and immediately was shocked. It was like his fingertips were pricked with sharp needles. Was that what she was feeling right now? He had to know, so he touched her cheek again.

He gritted his teeth against the needle poking feeling and reached out to her. She was in pain. That was the only feeling that was coming through their connection. He released her cheek and stared down at her.

He felt helpless. He didn't know what he could do. He stood and was about to go find someone, maybe his mother to help with this, but then he thought of something. When he was feeling sad the other day about his father, Eva had connected with him and sent him soothing thoughts. She made him feel better. Could he do that?

He stopped with his hand on the door. Instead of leaving his room, he closed the door. He turned back to Eva and swept her up in his arms. He strode over to the bed and laid her down. Her breathing was still shallow, and beads of sweat appeared on her scrunched brow.

This was it, he had to try. Jace took both his hands and laid them on either side of her head. The pain was there, but he tried to think of soothing thoughts to send to her.

It was hard for him to think since all he was getting was the pain. Her breath hitched and suddenly, she stopped breathing, the pain he was feeling stopped altogether. He looked down at her and realized what was happening.

He was starting to panic. He shook her shoulders slightly. "Eva!" She didn't respond and she wasn't breathing. He couldn't lose her. Not now. Not ever. He sat on the edge of the bed and gathered her up in his arms. "Eva," his voice cracked. He hadn't realized that tears formed in his eyes. He held her, one hand on the back of her neck the other wrapped around her waist. His forehead dropped to hers.

"Don't leave me. Breathe Eva. Breathe. I'll take your pain, just breathe." Several seconds went by as silent tears tumbled down his cheeks and onto Eva's face. Then he felt it, that needle stabbing pain. It was faint, but then grew. He felt Eva take a huge breath.

He sobbed in relief to hear that breath. But then the pain intensified as if it was coming to him. It was immense. It was like his insides were being stabbed repeatedly. He pushed through the pain and listened.

Eva's breathing sounded like music to his ears. He had no idea what was happening, but he knew that he wasn't going to let her go. Maybe he was doing exactly what he said he would do. Was he taking that pain from her?

He groaned. He leaned back in bed still holding Eva. If this was what she was experiencing, then he could understand what happened to her. He almost wanted to die too. But he gritted his teeth and would suffer through this. He didn't want her to have to take this pain again.

Amongst the painful stabs he held her tight to his chest, unwilling to let go. It was like she was his lifeline. He didn't know how much time passed. But soon, the pain pushed him into darkness.

He felt like he was run over by a bull. Jace was slowly waking up. He had this weird dream about Eva and how she came into his room and collapsed because she was in pain. He somehow took that away from her and then he succumbed to the pain. Yeah, it was bizarre.

He began to stretch when he realized he wasn't alone. He opened his eyes and stared down at the top of a dark-haired woman that was lying against his chest. Wait a second, was that dream real? He groaned and realized that what he wanted to be a dream, happened last night.

Eva was curled up sleeping against his chest. Her soft breath puffed against him. Her small hand splayed over his chest. Through the connection he could feel peace and contentment. He sighed, relieved that she was no longer in any pain. He had to ask her about that when she woke up.

He took his arms and wrapped them around her. It was interesting that she was still here, but then again last night wasn't any normal circumstance. He'd have to ask her what happened to her. Jace was wondering if he should just enjoy the moment, lying there snuggling with Eva, or get up.

"Jace," he heard through the door. Oh crap! That was his father's voice. He heard his footsteps stop outside his door. There was no time. His father spoke as he opened the door. "I just had this crazy thought this morning and wanted to," his father stopped speaking as soon as the door opened, and his gaze landed on Jace. His father's eyes widened and then his brow lowered. That wasn't good.

Jace's own eyes were wide in fear of what his father might be thinking. He glanced down at Eva, who seemed to not realize what was happening, since she was still asleep and then he looked back toward his father. Jace started to carefully move Eva off him. "Father, it's not what it looks like."

"Right," his father's look said he didn't believe him. It probably looked bad because Jace was shirtless.

"I can explain," he gave a pleading look to his father. He started to move off the bed so he could be as far away from Eva as possible.

"I expect that," his father's voice was stern. "As soon as possible. In my study." Before Jace could respond his father shut the door. He sat on the edge of the bed looking at the closed door. What was his father thinking right now? Obviously not good thoughts. He was in trouble. He put his hand over his face and slowly wiped down.

Soft rustling sounded next to him, and he turned his head to see Eva stretching out. Dear Fates, she was gorgeous. Her raven-colored hair was spread out around her, and her arms were above her head. He wasn't trying to notice but her soft womanly shape was outlined underneath her nightgown. He saw the smooth skin of her calves and her bare feet. His gaze travelled down and then back up.

Jace's eyes hooded over, and his heart started to beat just a little harder. He looked a bit long at her chest, his gaze settling on the precious gift he gave her nestled in the bunched cloth of her nightgown and then moved his eyes along the chain against her delicate skin of her neck and then to her lips. They had a slight smile and then he saw those piercing hazel eyes on him.

He turned away, embarrassed about being caught looking at her. He could see out of the corner of his eyes that she rose to a sitting position. "What time is it?" she asked.

"Morning," he dared a glance at her. She was looking about her slightly confused.

"How did I end up here?"

"You don't remember."

"I was awake last night. I went down the hall and then I," she shook her head from side to side, probably trying to figure out what she did.

"And you came to my room," he supplied. Her gaze locked with his, but she still looked confused.

"No."

"Well, you did. Because if you haven't noticed, that's where you are right now."

"That's weird."

"I know, usually you leave and sleep in your room, but here you were, sleeping right here when I woke up."

"Wait, what? Did you just say I was sleeping?"

"Yes."

"Are you sure?"

"I'm positive I know what sleeping looks like. Someone who is lying down, eyes closed, breathing even. Trust me, you were sleeping."

"Really?" She sat there looking off at nothing, like she was contemplating something.

"And it got me in trouble." He stood and walked over to a chair where his robe was discarded. He put the garment on and tied it off.

"Father decided to just walk on in this morning and there we were. Of course, you were still asleep, but it was embarrassing. I know we didn't do anything." He turned back to Eva, and he saw her wide eyed and staring at his chest with her mouth slightly open.

"You alright?" he asked. Her gaze met his and then she quickly looked away with a slight blush on her face.

"I'm sorry," she stammered. "That was not my intent."

"Well, let's not make matters worse. You should probably get back to your room." She nodded and slid off the bed. She made her way past him trying not to look at him. He touched her elbow and stopped her, "Eva, wait." She stopped and turned her head to look at him.

"Promise you'll talk with me before I leave," he said. She looked down as if thinking about it and then her gaze moved back to his.

"I promise." He smiled at her and released her elbow. She smiled back and turned and left the room. He closed his eyes for a moment, just to think.

Jace had to meet with his father, and he wasn't sure what he expected. All he could hope for was that his father would understand. He wouldn't do anything to harm Eva. He didn't understand what happened last night, but he did remember. He and Eva did not do anything. She was innocent.

His father was going to kill him.

Chapter 32
Eavesdropping

Eva had made sure that her pack was tucked away in the corner of the stables. After dressing earlier, she was totally caught off guard when Jace told her she had been sleeping. She never slept. It was such a shock to her it took her a second to try and figure out what happened.

She remembered going into the mayor's room and decided to help him out. The last thing she remembered was taking his pain. She only could guess that she somehow made it to Jace's room, and she fell asleep. Was it because she had to endure all the mayor's pain? That must have sapped her energy. She did have to say that now that she slept, she felt fantastic.

The only problem with sleeping was that she was now behind with what she wanted to accomplish. She had to carefully avoid people when she could have easily avoided them during the night. She thought she was caught twice, but she was able to slip in the shadows and the people walked by without even glancing her way.

Eva now had to go talk with Jace. She wasn't mad at him, not after seeing him this morning. Just the thought of his toned muscular back sent shivers down her spine and a warm glow spread throughout her body. What was that? She never felt like that before, and it made her feel embarrassed. Was she blushing just thinking about him?

She had to get her thoughts in order. It was getting close to midday already and she knew that he would soon be on his way. She just had to go find out where he was. She slinked out of the stables and was able to slip inside the kitchen door. Of course, at this time of day she would be noticed going through the kitchen, but that was a common occurrence for the kitchen staff.

As she was going down the hall toward the parlor, she heard a conversation taking place in the study. The study door was slightly ajar. She slowed and walked toward the door zoning in on the voices.

"Yes, I have everything I need." Eva recognized the voice as Jace.

"That's good to hear." The next was the mayor but he didn't sound happy. There was a lull in the conversation. Eva wondered what was going on. "Let's discuss what happened this morning," the mayor continued.

"Nothing happened."

"That's not what I saw."

"I know that it looked bad, but it really was nothing. She usually doesn't fall asleep in my room."

"It sounds like she's in your room a lot."

"I didn't mean it that way. She just visits me and then leaves."

"Visits you?" Eva heard Jace groan slightly. It didn't sound like he was convincing his father very well.

"Let me start over. Ever since she came here, she's always walked around at night. True?"

"Yes, I have caught her a few times doing that."

"Okay, well, sometimes she would stop in and talk."

"Talk?"

"Yes. She did it before I left for school, and she still does it now that I am back." Eva realized that Jace was talking about her. Was it wrong to go talk with Jace?

"That's it, you just talk?"

"Yes father. She doesn't stay long and then she goes back to her room or wherever. And I'm telling you that last night was the first time she didn't leave."

"I'm torn Jace. I want to believe you, but your mother was right. I can't believe I missed it."

"Father, believe me. Eva is innocent. I would only treat her with as much respect as a mayor's daughter." What were they talking about? She didn't believe she did anything wrong.

"You want me to forget that I saw her lying in your arms?" Um, Eva didn't remember that. Was he holding her while she slept? At the thought, a smile quirked her lips. It reminded her of when he protectively held her after Devon attacked her. She felt safe and warm. For some reason she wanted to know what it was like being held while sleeping. Was it the same feeling?

"I obviously can't ask you to do that. Why don't you just talk with her? I'm sure she doesn't even realize that it was an issue."

"You knew better."

"Yes, I'll admit that. But, last night, it was, well. It's hard to explain. I fell asleep and before I knew it, I was waking up and you came into my bedroom. I was just as shocked as you at finding her in my bed." Oh, that was the issue? Was Eva not supposed to be in Jace's bed? Oh! A memory of a few months ago popped into her mind.

Eva was sitting with Lady Jebrow and her daughters while doing some needlework. It wasn't her favorite activity, but she indulged them by participating. Sasha and Sonya were gossiping as usual and were discussing a young man from town.

"I would sneak off with him," Sonya said and giggled.

"Sonya!" Lady Jebrow was shocked. "I will not here such things from you dear."

"I wouldn't do that mother," she feigned innocence.

"You are the mayor's daughter. Expectations for your behavior are held at a high level. You are not to be seen with the opposite sex without a chaperone."

"But Lucy goes and visits Wesley all the time by herself," Sasha whined.

"And what do you think will happen to Lucy? If they are found in a compromising position, Wesley will have to ask for her hand in marriage."

"Mom, Wesley is married. And it's not to Lucy," Sonya explained. Her mother's mouth dropped open, and she was floundering on what to say.

"Don't worry mom, we wouldn't do what Lucy would do," Sasha tried reassuring her.

"Of course, you will not! Now listen here you two." She turned her head toward Eva. "And you as well. You are not to be found in another man's bed that isn't your husband's. You shouldn't be in anyone else's bed period! I will be most upset

that you just gave yourself away. You are a sacred gift to your husband, and I will not have you girls throw that gift away to the first handsome boy you meet!"

"Gift?" Eva asked. She was confused at what Lady Jebrow was talking about. Lady Jebrow turned to her and softened her look.

"Eva, it was what we discussed a few years ago when you first became a woman. The act of procreation. You remember that information dear?" Eva nodded her head.

"Well, the act I am talking about should only happen between a husband and wife. You two have also heard this information," Lady Jebrow pointed at her daughters. "I expect all of you to behave and not stress out your father and me. You should be courted the proper way and hold onto your special gift. Got it?"

"Yes mother," the twins chimed.

Did the mayor think that she had committed the act with Jace? She didn't, he wouldn't. She would have known. There were signs that the deed was done and those were not present when they woke. Jace was telling his father the truth, she was innocent. They both were.

"What am I to do?" the major asked.

"If it will make it right, I'll take her hand in marriage." What? Did Eva just hear Jace correctly?

"Son, you put me in a tough position. I view you both as my children. She is as much a daughter to me as your sisters are." Eva's heart warmed at the mayor's words. "I haven't realized that you two had feelings for each other."

"What? I mean, I guess so."

"Are you saying you don't love Eva?"

"Um, no, I think." She heard the mayor chuckle. "I want to make it right. I don't want to disgrace her in any way."

"I'm sorry I find this situation funny. It just reminds me of the stupid things I did when it concerned your mother. Look, I won't tell anyone what I saw, but I want you to promise me that when you return from your trip that we discuss this further."

"Yes father."

"Have a safe journey son. Don't forget to say goodbye to your mother on the way out." Eva heard footsteps come to the door. She was too engrossed in the conversation she didn't move away in time. The door swung open and out walked Jace, right into her.

He stumbled slightly back and she as well, trying to orient themselves. His eyes widened when they landed on her. "Eva."

"Jace. You wanted to talk with me, remember?" She hoped that it didn't look like she was eavesdropping. She would have been very embarrassed if he found out that she was.

"Yes, I did." He looked back in the room, and she saw over his shoulder that the mayor was looking at them with a raised eyebrow. "Walk with me." He started off down the hall and Eva kept an even stride next to him.

He led them to the sliding door and stepped outside. He was silent as he made his way down to the pond. He stopped at the water's edge and looked out across its surface.

"I know you've been avoiding me because of this whole thing with me leaving." He stood there with his hands in his pockets. "And I realized that I haven't properly explained why." He turned toward her with a soft smile. "I'm going because I need to find out about the Child prophesy."

"Child prophesy?"

"Yes, it is a prophesy about a child of the Mighty that will bring light to the darkness."

"Where did you hear this prophesy?" Eva looked into his eyes, seeing the swirling green beneath the blue.

"I wish I could say. But you must believe me that I am only looking for information and will return as soon as I'm finished. I won't be gone long."

"Then let me come with you."

"Eva," he sighed.

"Jace. I need to come with you." Just after she said that a vision appeared.

The tied man, still waiting and wanting to continue his mission. The image shifted to the stars twinkling overhead, lingering on a certain constellation. Below the sky lay a mountain range where ancient people made their homes among the earth.

The vision was only brief but when she blinked Jace was holding onto her shoulders and deeply looking into her eyes.

"Tell me, tell me what you saw," he whispered. That crazy tug came, compelling her to tell him, that it was okay to let Jace know. She shook her head of the thought. He took it as her saying no.

"Eva, I know what you are."

"What?"

"I know you're a Seer."

"A Seer?" She didn't know what that was.

"Yes. It is an individual that can see visions. You just had a vision."

"How, how did you know?" This had never happened before. No one ever noticed when she had a vision. Did something happen when she had one?

"Nanna was a Seer."

"She was?"

"Yes, and her eyes did the same thing when she was having one of her visions."

"My eyes. What is going on with my eyes?"

"They turn completely white." Oh, wow. She didn't know. He saw her have a vision. He knew what it was, and he knew about Seers.

"I have to go with you Jace."

"Is it because of your vision?"

"It is."

"Tell me what you saw."

"I don't understand it. I just want you to trust me Jace. Please trust me that I must go with you. I must. It's important." Jace dropped his hands from her shoulders and ran a hand through his hair.

"Father will kill me," he mumbled. He locked his gaze with her thinking, assessing. Probably trying to figure out if this was a good idea. "Fine. But I'm leaving in fifteen minutes. I don't want it to make it look like you are coming with me, so, leave just after me and head in the opposite direction toward the west gate. I'll meet you at the rundown house in the field." The house where she took him one night with the magical flowers.

"I'll be there."

"I can't believe I'm allowing this. Don't tell anyone. I'll leave a note to be handed to father after dinner so that way he won't be able to do anything about it. And, well, we'll be in trouble when we get back."

"I don't care. I need to do what I am supposed to do." He sighed and quirked a smile.

"I guess I'm stuck with you, huh?"

"You won't ever get rid of me." She smiled at that. That fact that he trusted her to come with him, that was awesome. He also had information that she had to know. Maybe it will help her understand herself.

Chapter 33
Seers

They moved him into a room with a bed and a chair, but his feet were bound in chains connected to the wall. Number 034 shuffled over to the bed and sat down on the edge. His gaze fixed to the opening of the room. It seemed like wherever he was, the rooms did not have doors. The tightly packed earth around him made him believe he was possibly underground. The air was cool, and he was constantly shivering.

He wasn't told any of their names, except for the white-haired woman with light blue eyes. Her name was Willow. It took a few times of meeting her to finally figure out her Might power. Of course, she was a Seer, but all Seers have ability. She was a Controller. They were extremely rare. A Controller had the power over mind, making people do as they wished. That's why he felt compelled to stay, because she wanted him to stay.

It was no use trying to plot a way out of this place. Even if they released the chains on his feet, he still wouldn't be able to navigate his way out. He didn't know how far underground they were.

At least they gave him a lantern, which currently sat on the table. It lit the meager contents of the room, and he would turn it on and off as he chose. It didn't matter if it was on or off to know an individual was coming, since the hallway beyond the opening was always dark.

The hallway faintly glowed, showing that a person was approaching. Soon a cloaked individual appeared beyond the candle they held. It was Willow. He could tell by her soft tread and her movements. She entered the room and set her candle on the table. She pulled out the chair and set it in front of him. She gracefully sat and lowered her hood, letting her long silver hair flow over her shoulders and her blue piercing eyes be visible to the light.

"Willow," he started, "I assume you're here to extract more information from me?" It was what she always did. She would use her power to make him tell her things. Of course, the information she truly wanted was of the One, but he had very little information himself on the subject and she became frustrated every time with him. He couldn't tell her what he didn't know. It's not like he was a Seer.

"Why did you leave Brosch Stronghold?" A tingling feeling raced up his spine. It was hard in the darkness to see her aura, but he was sure it was pulsing around her. She compelled him to speak.

"I was told to, by a Seer."

"A Seer in Brosch's employ."

"We're not employed by Brosch. We are enslaved," he said through gritted teeth. It was not his choice to assist him in any way. He was just used like all the other Numbered.

"Then why continue to help him? Why not revolt against him?"

"Very few of us are together at any given time. It's like he knows what would happen if he did that."

"So, this Seer. How did she come to tell you?"

"Well, Brosch didn't know that the Seer was talking about me."

"How do you mean?"

"I was in the room to, well, do whatever Brosch was wanting me to do, and she happened to be in the room. All Seers are guarded twenty-four seven. In case of prophesy."

"You're a Healer."

"Yes." He wasn't surprised that she would know that. It did take some time to learn how to detect auras, but it could be done. He taught himself how to see them and understand them, even though it was forbidden to learn this trait in Brosch's Stronghold. Willow probably learned it before the Great War from another Might. It was entirely possible that they still practiced it outside of Brosch Stronghold.

"You were there to heal Brosch? Why would he need healing?" He closed his eyes, trying to refrain from giving too much information. What did it matter if they knew about him anyway? But there was this wall where it concerned Brosch. Every time Willow asked anything about him, it was like Number 034 was unable to tell her. It was frustrating for both, her because he didn't tell her and him because her power was causing him pain.

"I can't," he groaned, squinting in pain. "I'm sorry, it's not within my power to tell you." He felt her power release and he breathed deeply, grateful that she didn't suffocate him.

"It's interesting, how he still holds some control. Do you know why that is?" He just shook his head in response. "You were saying that Brosch didn't know she was speaking about you, but you did. Did this Seer prophesize?"

"Yes. She had a prophesy while I was in the room. Of course, as soon as it became apparent that she was speaking, he had me dismissed from the room. But her prophesy was not long, she was done before I was pushed out the door."

"What did she say?"

"I don't remember verbatim, but she said, 'The sun's orange rays set in clear skies. Thirty-four will go, one will come. The Child will see into death and learn to become One,' or something like that."

"And how did you know she was talking about you?"

"I am thirty-four, 034. If I go, then One will come. I didn't know that I was going to be going on some grand mission to find the actual One."

"What about this Child reference? What do you make of that?"

"I can only assume that the Child is the One. That he became the One when exposed to death."

"Interesting theory, for a Healer."

"If you can interrupt this prophesy better than I can, Seer, then do so. I've told you what I know. And as I told you before, I have no idea who the One is. Not until I see him with my own eyes will I know."

"I had a vision, Numbered. We will be visited by two. I gathered from the vision that one was seeking me and the other seeking you. Why would that be?"

"I have told you already. I have information the One will need to bring Brosch to his knees."

"Yet you can't even tell me about him, since he somehow created around you a barrier, blocking you from even giving up details about him. What person of Might did he use to create this?" Willow was more talking to herself at this point. She knew that he would not be able to say the answer even if he knew. Anything tied with Brosch was blocked.

Willow stood and moved the chair back to the table and took the candle. She turned to him with a warm smile, like she always did. "I will send you a meal shortly. Sleep well, Numbered." She turned from him and left the room.

If her vision was right, the One was on his way here. Number 034 prayed that he would get here before the Chasers found him.

Chapter 34
Gene Newly

"There it is, Newly Stronghold," Jace said pointing off toward the north. It had been a pleasant ride so far. They camped out the first night and made great time today. It was evening and they were already arriving at their destination.

"Do you think he will remember me?" Eva asked.

"I don't know. You've changed a lot. In a good way." He glanced over at Eva whose hair cascaded down her back in a long braid and swung with the motion of the horse. Her skin was rosy from the sun's rays and her eyes seemed bright with excitement yet tinged with a hint of weariness.

They made their way through Newly's village just outside the walls. His people were thriving. His stronghold had to have taken a blow from the Great War and probably had to be rebuilt like his father's stronghold. Newly was just a boy when the Great War took place fifteen years ago. His father had died during the Battle of Wedset. The battle took place at the foot of the Wedset Mountains. It was the turning point of the war. Many lives were lost, including Newly's father.

Along the top of the stronghold walls, Jace noticed several men, each with a bow on his back. Sentinels patrolling. Not a bad idea. He and Eva made their way to the south gate where two more Sentinels stood. They must have not posed a threat since they easily made their way into the city.

He led his horse along the cobblestone streets toward the east side of the city. It had been some time since he was here last, but he remembered visiting as a boy and was sure that the mayor's home was over on this side. Eva trotted along behind him, since the streets were full of merchants where only one horse at a time could squeeze through.

The crowds finally cleared as they came upon the mayor's home. It was large, as to be expected, with four stone pillars two-stories high adorning the front. Jace remembered the fountain in the square before reaching the mayor's home and when he was a boy, he dipped his feet in and played in the water. Now he saw a few mothers sitting together there and their children were doing just that, splashing their feet in the water.

Once they reached the steps that led to the entrance, he dismounted from his horse. Eva followed suit. He whistled and a boy came from who knows where and stopped in front of him.

"How can I be of service sir?" the small boy asked. He had a few smudges but looked well fed.

"Hold these two horses for us. As soon as we are admitted, have them taken to the mayor's stables," he took two coins from his pocket and handed them to the boy.

"Absolutely sir," the boy responded bowing his head. Jace looked over at Eva and cocked his head in the direction of the entrance. She followed him up the stairs. Once they reached the top, two men guarded either side of the door.

Jace stopped in front of one man and dug into his pocket. He removed a card and handed it to the man. The guard took the card, looked at it, and turned toward the door. The guard opened it and went inside, without inviting them in.

"What'd you hand him?" Eva asked at this side.

"It has my name on it."

"Is that standard?"

"Depends. I'm sure Newly is expecting us, but I think we arrived early. We made pretty good time."

"Will they let me in? I didn't give them a card."

"You're with me. You'll get in." They waited a few more minutes and then the guard finally came back.

"The mayor is expecting you Mr. Jebrow. Please follow me." The guard motioned for Jace to enter. Jace crossed the threshold ahead of the guard. "I'm sorry miss, you are not allowed," the guard stopped Eva.

"She's with me," Jace told the guard.

"She is not expected. Only people that are expected are allowed into the mayor's home sir." Jace turned back toward the door to see Eva blocked by the guard's arm and her eyebrow raised. He stepped back toward them and looked at the guard.

"She's allowed. Let her in." The guard hesitated just briefly but then dropped his arm. Eva looked from the guard to Jace with a scrunched brow. She tentatively took a step forward. The guard didn't move, and she shrugged and continued on. They both moved along the entrance way.

"Told you," Jace said under his breath to her. They stopped in the middle of the room and looked around the grand entrance. A curving staircase led up to the second floor. A chandelier hung two stories down and looked to be lit by at least a hundred candles.

"That's a little bit extravagant," Jace heard Eva mumble.

"I don't know, I think it fits with the décor." Eva just shook her head. The guard stepped in front of them and led the rest of the way. They didn't go very far, just on the other side of the large staircase. The guard opened the double door and stood to the side.

Jace and Eva stepped into the room. Jace wasn't allowed in this room when he visited last, so he didn't recognize it. A large desk sat in the center with a few chairs in front. Floor to ceiling windows were just behind the desk. There was a man sitting at the desk looking over some papers. Jace could only assume that it was Newly.

Jace and Eva came close to the desk and Newly lifted his head to look at them. He stood and came around his desk holding out his hand toward Jace.

"Jace Jebrow." He took Jace's hand and shook it. "Wow. The last time I saw you, you were a little boy." He dropped his hand back to his side and sized Jace up. "You definitely are your father's son."

"Yeah, you just look older sir." The man laughed and shook his head.

"Well, if I changed too much then nobody would know who I was." He crossed his arms and leaned on the front of his desk. "You've arrived earlier than I thought you would."

"We made good time sir," Jace glanced at Eva. She was staring at Newly, waiting. Newly finally turned his gaze toward her, acknowledging that there was another person besides Jace. He looked like he was going to ignore her, but his brow furrowed, and he looked back at her. He blinked a few times and then a slow smile crept on his face.

"I say," Newly spoke. "Is this the same girl I found in the tower seven years ago?" Eva took a step forward and lowered her gaze.

"Thank you for saving me," she quietly said.

"She speaks!" Newly laughed to himself and moved to stand in front of her. "Let me look at you properly." She raised her head slowly so that Newly could study her face. If a smile could be brighter than the sun, then Newly definitely displayed that now. "Yes, those hazel eyes. How could I forget?"

"Eva was anxious about seeing you again, since she is not the same little girl," Jace explained.

"Clearly! She's not little anymore. She's almost the same height as me." Newly was tall, but Jace was still taller. Jace guessed he was around six feet. "This is a most pleasant surprise. And Eva did you say?"

"Yes, indeed sir," Jace answered.

"Beautiful name. Now, as excited as I am to catch up with both of you, we will have to postpone our discussion until after supper." Newly moved off to sit behind his desk once again. He continued, "Your father of course did not give me any details in the letter as to why you wanted to visit, not about Eva visiting either."

"Well, it was a last-minute decision for Eva to come," Jace explained.

"I don't know if that decision was good, but it was a surprise, and a pleasant one at that. And the reason for your visit Jebrow?"

"To find the Rens location."

"Ah," Newly nodded his head. "Like I said, a discussion that can take place after supper. My man Winston here will see you to your rooms," he gestured to a servant that had been standing to the side of the room. Jace didn't even know he was there to begin with he was so silent.

"Thank you, sir," Jace said with a bow.

"Supper is in an hour. I think that is plenty of time for you both to freshen up from your travels," Newly smiled at both, lingering his gaze on Eva.

"Yes," she softly answered. Winston gestured for them to follow but Eva must have not been paying attention, still staring at Newly. What was up with her?

Jace softly touched her shoulder, "Eva." She blinked a few times and looked at Jace. She must have realized she was staring and gave a shaky smile to Newly and let Jace lead her out of the room. The two of them followed the servant up the grand staircase.

"What was that about?" Jace asked out the side of his mouth to Eva.

"I don't think it's a good time to discuss it now." Something was causing that scrunched brow of hers. They were going to talk about it later.

"Here is the lady's room," Winston said and stopped in front of the door. He opened it and from his view Jace could see it was a well-furnished room. He hoped he wasn't too far away from her.

Eva stepped into the room and turned back toward Jace. "I'll see you down at supper?"

"Of course. I'll come to escort you down," Jace reassured her.

"Okay." She slowly started to close the door and just before it latched, she smiled at him.

"This way sir," Winston said, jogging him out of his thoughts. He followed the servant the rest of the way to the room he would be staying in. He just had this strange feeling that he shouldn't leave Eva's side, which was absurd. He needed to get his feelings in check, or he might do something he would regret later.

Chapter 35
The Location

"Marvelous meal with great company. I hope you have enjoyed yourself as much as I." Eva smiled politely at Gene. He was a gracious host and reminded her of the time he was very generous toward her. If she knew that Jace was going to his stronghold, she would have brought something to repay him for the time and money he spent on her. It was the least she could do.

"Yes, thank you sir, it was exquisite," Jace said at her side. Jace cleaned up nice, wearing a nice form-fitted dark green jacket and crisp clean shirt. She could smell his wonderful scent that reminded her of rainstorms and forests. He was attentive towards her this evening. If he was any closer, they would have bumped elbows.

"And how about you Eva, was the food satisfactory?" Gene asked.

"Of course. It was wonderful."

"I'm glad. Now, Jebrow I believe we need to retire to my study to discuss the reason you came." Gene stood and Jace with him. Eva stood too which drew Gene's attention. "Oh, Eva there is no need for you to join us."

"I disagree," she said.

"Really?" Gene cocked an eyebrow.

"I will be traveling with Jace, so it is apparent that I am also present for this conversation."

"No, no, no. I am not going to let you go chasing after the Rens like young Jebrow plans on doing." This was absurd. Jace knew that she had to come. Of course, it would be hard to try and persuade Gene, but if anyone could do it, Jace could.

"Jace?" Eva looked at him for assistance.

"Sir, I don't think Eva being in the room will be much different than if she was out. I'll be telling her anyways." Gene crossed his arms looking at him with a slightly stern expression.

"And why would you do that?" Gene asked.

"As she said, she will be traveling with me." Gene did not like that answer. He looked to be mulling it over and then he conceded.

"Fine. Follow me." He made his way out of the dining room down the hall to his study. Once inside Gene went to a cabinet and pulled out a glass and a flask of dark liquid. He poured two fingers worth in the glass and took it and drank it down in one gulp.

Jace had settled in one of the chairs in front of Gene's desk, so Eva decided to sit in the other, waiting for Gene to join.

Gene filled his glass again, this time bringing the glass with him as he settled in his chair behind his desk. "So, you want to know where the Rens are?" Gene asked.

"We do," Jace answered.

"Of course, I must inquire why, since I just can't give up their location. It could put their lives in danger, you understand."

"I seek a Seer. My father told me that there was one underground, and she was with the Rens."

"What do you need a Seer for?" Jace thinned his lips. He obviously didn't like sharing his plans. But this was Gene, he was good. Eva would know if he wasn't. His aura was just how she remembered, a soft green color. Although it was pulsing slightly just like earlier. She wasn't used to seeing auras do that. The Jebrow family had bright auras, but none of them pulsed. She would have to think on that later what that meant. For now, she knew that she could trust Gene.

"He seeks to learn more about the Child prophesy," Eva told him. Jace snapped his gaze to her silently asking why she would give him that information.

"Interesting prophesy. I've heard rumors of one about some Child that will overthrow Brosch. That would be nice." Gene sipped his drink and set the glass on the desk's surface. "So, I am guessing you have heard this prophesy Jebrow?"

"I have."

"From a Seer?" Jace tensed slightly at the question. He didn't immediately answer, and Eva noticed a small smile creep up on Gene's face. "Now, that is some interesting information." Wait, did Gene think that Jace heard that prophesy from a Seer? When had he met a Seer?

Then it dawned on Eva. She was a Seer. He had seen her when she had a vision. Was it possible that she also said a prophesy? She didn't remember saying anything about a Child and what not.

"I must find another Seer to confirm," Jace explained. Another Seer he said. Gene must have picked up on that too.

"What is your Seer's name? I only know of one Seer that has not been captured by Brosch. All the others are in his stronghold."

"I'm not saying." It was her. Eva was the Seer he was talking about. Why didn't he mention that it was she that said the prophesy? When did she say it?

"You're protecting her. Just like the Rens are protecting their Seer. The Rens are a small group but are fierce. They never stay in one place too long. A Seer is their only safe bet that they remain underground, away from Brosch. Of course, I know where they are, because I give them people they can train. People with the Might."

"Yes, you and Holds do extraordinary work, extricating people that were taken by Brosch. But that doesn't mean I have to trust you, just like you don't have to trust me." What was Jace trying to do? If he continued with this route, they wouldn't get their answer.

Gene smiled and he looked down into his drink glass. His aura pulsed and Eva could tell it was because he was thinking of something. "I tell you what." Gene continued, "You tell me who your Seer is, and I'll tell you where the Rens are."

Jace sat there, having a staring competition with Gene. Eva looked back and forth between the two men. She didn't think anything was going to come of this battle. Neither of them knew about the vision she had about the constellation and the mountain range. She knew that was her destination, and if Gene wasn't going to give the information up, she will just have to go by her vision and hope for the best.

Eva stood and drew the attention of both men. She smiled as sweetly as she could at Gene. "It was only a courtesy that we asked you Gene where the Rens were. We already know where they are." She wasn't surprised that both men gave her a questioning look.

"Really? And how is that? From the Seer Jace speaks of? Did she know?"

"Maybe."

"What do you mean by maybe?"

"All she told us was a direction. She didn't specifically tell us what we would find, just that it was somewhere we needed to go." Dawning shown on Jace's face.

"So, then why the need to come to me?" That was a good question. Why did they have to come to Gene then? She knew that they needed to be here first, but she didn't know why she got that feeling.

"It is obvious, isn't it?" Jace asked. "You are on the way." Eva watched as Gene pursed his lips and shook his head. He sighed and leaned back in his seat.

"Your father doesn't know about the Seer, does he?"

"You truly hold up to your reputation sir." Jace continued, "My father told me to come to you. However, it was not needed. Would I not trust my father? I came, just as he said I should."

"Indeed." Gene turned to Eva with a smile. "I think that you've made your point clear. I will be happy to assist you the remainder of your journey. I think an early night will do us all good."

Jace finally rose and came over to Eva. He held out his arm for her to take. She placed her hand in the crook of his arm to be led out. "We appreciate the help sir. Good night." Jace slightly bowed his head.

"Good night," Eva also said. Jace steered her out of the room.

Once they were out of ear shot, Jace leaned over and said, "We definitely need to talk, tonight." He kept going, taking them up the stairs. "Come find me in my room when everyone else is asleep."

"So, like usual," she smiled. He smiled back at her.

"Yep, like usual."

Chapter 36
Breathe

Jace woke suddenly. He sat up and looked around him. It took him a moment to remember that he was not in his own room. He rubbed his forehead. There was a slight pounding feeling, like a small man was beating on the inside of his skull. That must have been what made him wake.

It wasn't the only thing he was feeling. He felt this tug, like a pull coming from his chest. That was weird. He was still a little groggy, but he decided that a little bit of water might help. He removed his covers and stood up. He took a robe and slipped it on, tying it in place around his waist. He yawned and shuffled to the nightstand.

Before he could reach it, the tug in his chest felt like it wanted him to leave the room. He stared at the door then glanced at the water. His head was getting slightly worse, so it was hard for him to concentrate. He moved toward the door and opened it. Once he stepped out in the hall the pull took him toward the opposite end of the hall from the grand staircase.

Jace was curious, but it seemed like the tug was now beyond his control. It was like he needed to go, or he was going to be torn in half. His feet led him directly to the end of the hall where there was a door. He opened it and a set of stairs lay beyond. It was dark and he immediately regretted not taking a candle with him. He still ascended the steps. The pull was starting to get stronger.

At the top of the steps was another door, which he pushed open. He stepped out into the cool air. He looked to be standing atop the mayor's home. Stars shone down and the moon was half full hanging high in the sky. The tug took him toward the edge of the roof. Jace looked out and could see just beyond the stronghold wall. This would be a good lookout point. He went to the right and the pull was even stronger, but his head was also pounding to the point that he started to squint.

He shook his head and kept moving forward, closer to the pull in his chest. He went several steps when he noticed a crumpled figure on the narrow path. He moved closer as both his chest and head pulled toward the individual.

Jace knelt and turned the figure toward the moon's glow. He sucked in a breath seeing who it was.

He gathered Eva in his arms, seeing that her eyes were closed, and her mouth was hanging open. She was limp and he had a sense that he was experiencing the same episode as the other night.

"Eva," he said to her. He checked to see if she was breathing, and he could feel nothing. "Eva!" he choked. He touched the back of her neck and brought his forehead to hers. "Eva, breathe! You must breathe." If only the pounding in his head would subside enough for him to concentrate.

He looked down at her face. Seeing her lit up in the moonlight it reminded him of the time when she was surrounded by those glowing flowers. He grazed his thumb over her bottom lip and was tempted. He wasn't thinking right. But he had a thought just then. If she wasn't breathing, maybe he could breathe for her. It was a crazy notion, but what other choice did he have?

Jace brought his lips to hers. She of course was not conscious, so her lips remained motionless. He concentrated through the pounding in his head and breathed. He thought of her lungs filling with air. He would give her anything she needed, if she stayed alive.

He no longer felt the tug. Instead, he felt it reverse, as if he was pushing it out. He wanted to give her his life. He knew in that moment, lips on hers, that he would die for this woman.

He felt a tingling feeling all over his body. That feeling he was pushing out, was now pushing back at him. He held on, trying to focus with his pounding head. He then felt the two pulses merge. He still felt like he was pushing, but he was also receiving something. The air that he had pushed into Eva's lungs was now being pushed back.

He released her lips and stared down at her. The pounding in his head slowly subsided down into this inner pulse he felt in his chest. It was weird, like he was tied now. Her eyes popped open, and he sighed in relief.

Jace crushed her to his chest and held her against him, unwilling to let her go. He felt her hands come up and grasp his elbows. He pulled back to look down into her hazel eyes.

"Jace." He felt in his chest along that thread a feeling of safety, comfort and warmth. Was that Eva he was feeling?

"Eva," he gently said and smoothed back some of her hair from her forehead. It was odd, but he didn't feel any connection through his touch, it seemed like he was already feeling it, if that were possible. "Are you alright?"

"I, I guess so."

"Here, let me help you." He stood and helped her stand with him. She shakily stood and gripped his arms for assistance. She looked around and then up at him with wide eyes. There was that feeling again in his chest, knowing that she was also feeling the same as he.

"What is that?" she asked.

"I have no idea."

"Is it, our connection?"

"Maybe. Are you good to stand on your own?"

"Yeah." She let go of him and stood, brushing off some debris that ended up on her. Odd, he still felt the connection, even without holding her. He felt that she was nervous and a slight bit scared but safe.

"What were you doing up here?"

"Oh, I was just getting some fresh air."

"Right," he felt that she was holding something back. She looked at him pleadingly.

"Can I explain it to you later?" He felt that she was tired. He could let her get some sleep then, but they were going to talk in the morning.

"Here," he held out his hand to her. She took it and warmth spread through him. She liked holding his hand. Well, he'll have to remember that for next time. They silently made their way back to the stairway and inside. They moved to his door, and he was going to continue on to her room, but he could feel that she was hesitant.

"I know it's not proper," she began, "but can I stay with you?" Her eyes locked onto his. She didn't want to be alone and if he were honest, he didn't want her out of his sight.

"Sure." He pushed open the door and led her inside. She released his hand and made her way over to the bed. He closed the door and this time made sure a lock was secured in place. As he turned back toward the bed, he saw that she already shed the robe that she was wearing. The light of the moon shone through the window, and he caught a glimpse of her curves through her nightgown.

Heat seared within him. He had to get his thoughts under control. He closed his eyes and took slow breaths. When he opened his eyes, she was already in the bed with the covers over her. He was sure that if he could feel her erratic emotions, that she was feeling his.

Jace slowly made his way on the other side of the bed. He took off his own robe and slipped under the covers. The heat wouldn't let up. He lied there, staring up at the ceiling, painfully aware that Eva lay next to him. He tried to focus on the feeling in his chest. He felt contentment and peace. He glanced over at her and could hear her even breathing. She was already asleep.

She was curled on her side away from him. He was so tempted to touch her, to know that she was safe. He stared at her long hair for who knows how long contemplating the decision to wrap his arm around her. He drifted off to sleep and dreamed of his dark-haired beauty.

Chapter 37
Found Out

Eva was putting the last items in her travel sack so they could continue their journey. Something happened last night between her and Jace and it laid heavy on her mind.

The reason she was outside last night was to look at the constellations, since remembering the vision she had, she wanted to locate it. She had found the same image among the stars, knowing that the mountain range that spread out in her vision was where they needed to go, and the stars would guide them. Well, at least that was where *she* needed to go.

While atop the mayor's home she looked out beyond the walls, taking in the surrounding area. At first it was peaceful, standing there in the dark. But as she looked, she saw a flicker of an aura that she thought she'd never see again.

She waited there, watching the aura move closer. He wasn't the only one. Two more approached from opposite sides, their color a dull remnant of what it once was. She associated these auras as an enemy. Memories filled her mind of the red-robed men and the guards that fed her once and awhile or abused her. Each of their auras were tainted, as if by going through with their hateful acts caused hope to leave the recesses of their minds and pollute their very essence.

The three figures met and were in discussion. She was too far away to hear their words, but she knew that something was going on. One gestured toward his hounds, which each of them had two, and then around him. The other two nodded their heads and did some of the same gesturing.

Eva was curious. She was so focused on their conversation that she started to *hear* it. It startled her for a moment, but she was so fascinated by it, that she just let it happen.

What she heard was that the hounds picked up a Might signature. They were discussing where each of them had picked up this signature and what their next move was. The end decision was to enter the stronghold, since it seemed that the signature passed through every gate.

She didn't know what she was doing until it was already happening. She wanted more information on the hounds and what these men's mission was. Somehow, she broke into each mind, extracting the information, learning that they were Chasers and how the hounds picked up Might signature, and the actual person they were after.

It was such an overload of information, like she had extracted all their memories. Horrible images came into her mind. They tortured people, some even to death. They did these acts without remorse. It boiled her blood and a huge well of anger built inside her.

Eva reached out along that invisible thread and was able to wrap around each Chaser's Spark. Their Sparks were black as death. She wrenched them away, knowing that once a Spark was taken, it could never be returned. She knew what she had done, but she couldn't chance them getting into the stronghold and finding her.

She felt drained and collapsed where she stood. Their tortured victims were playing over and over in her mind, and she was suffocating from the intensity of death. There was no hope, the world was doomed.

And yet, there was a light that pierced the fogginess of her mind. It was a hand reaching out, showing the way out. She grasped on, accepting the warm feeling that spread throughout, lifting the darkness away. When she opened her eyes Jace's face was there with those piecing blues seeming to stare into the depths of her soul.

Now, as Eva swung her pack on her back, she could feel Jace. It was this constant pulse in her chest, like their hearts beat together. Now he was anxious. She felt the same, since she wanted to leave as soon as possible. She rubbed her chest, but of course the action wasn't going to help his feelings leave her.

She made her way down the large staircase and was going to head out to the stables to ready their horses. She had slept again, but thankfully this time for not as long. She woke next to Jace, where his arm had found its way around her and his warmth seeped into her like a fire. She was able to leave without waking him and began preparing for their departure.

Before she reached the door Gene called out to her, "Eva." She stopped and turned her head and saw him come up to her in long strides. He had a friendly smile on his face, but his eyes showed slight weariness. Something was on his mind. "Leaving so soon?" He pointed to her pack.

"Oh, no I was just getting everything around is all."

"Good, because I would like to discuss something with you. Can you come to my study?"

"Sure," she shrugged. She followed him back to the large study. It looked different with the morning light shining in, not as foreboding and inviting. Gene moved behind his desk and sat. He motioned for her to have a seat.

Eva moved toward one of the chairs and realized she still had her pack on her back. She took it off and set it next to the chair. As she was removing her pack, she noticed Gene's aura was pulsing again. Some bit of information floated to the surface of her mind. The hounds tracked Might signature. They could only do that if a person with Might was using their ability.

She lowered her pack and sat slowly in her chair. Gene placed his hands together in his lap and leaned back in his chair. "There has always been this question in the back of my mind. It has to do with when Holds and I found you in the tower." Ah, the question, the one about the guards that Mayor Jebrow asked about. "I was curious about the guards that we came upon. It's not like we were planning on finding the tower in the first place, so we didn't feel the need to look deeper into their deaths. But there is one thing I remember."

"And what is that?" she softly asked. She had a strange sense that she knew exactly what he would say. He leaned closer looking at her intently.

"The looks on their faces. I never forgot it." Gene stood and started to move out and around his desk. "And it just so happens that I have seen these deathly expressions again." He stopped in front of her. She didn't want to look up, but she did anyway. His aura wasn't pulsing any longer but spreading out. Her eyes were wide as she was able to see a small tendril skim the surface of her skin. It was, interesting. She looked down at her hand mesmerized by the sensation.

Then it hit her. That was the same feeling she got from Jace, when he was telling her to do something. This compulsion wanted her to clear her mind and be able to see different paths within her decisions. She blocked the feeling like she did with Jace. Gene continued unaware of her reactions.

"Of course, I'm sure that you have heard about the Chasers that were seen close by my stronghold. I've had to be extra careful lately, not being able to go and complete any missions. Do you know what my Sentinels found this morning? Three dead Chasers. All of them with that expression. So, I asked myself, what would cause this expression? I've only seen it one other time. It got me thinking. You must have done something, Eva. You are the only constant between the tower and this incident. It cannot be coincidence."

Eva lifted her gaze to Gene. Did he know? She didn't even have to say anything.

"It's hard for me to understand it though," he continued, moving away to the side of the room where a table that had a map spread out on its surface. "There were no reports of you leaving the stronghold last night, which means you stayed here, in my home. At the tower, you were in a locked dungeon." He turned back to her, his aura changed back to just pulsing and not spreading around the room as it was. She saw some color linger in the air. "I think I know why Brosch would put a little girl in a tower. And I understand why I should probably fear her."

"They were not tracking me."

"Right, sure they weren't." He didn't believe her.

"You know they weren't. They were tracking a Numbered that had escaped." She learned this when she extracted information from the Chasers.

"That's the closest they have been to the wall."

"Because the hounds were tracking a Might signature." His brow scrunched.

"I've heard that they can do that."

"But the hounds cannot distinguish between the different signatures, only that they have found one." Eva was getting the idea of which Might signature they had picked up.

"Are you saying the Numbered escapee was outside my wall? Possibly walked around my city?"

"No, the signature is like a scent they would track. It doesn't stay forever, it fades. The hounds were tracking a recent signature and it wasn't the Numbered."

"Yours?"

"No, not mine. I wouldn't know what mine looks like anyway. I don't think I can see my own." His eyes widened and a smile tweaked in the corner of his mouth.

"You can see people with the Might. I've met people that can do this and it's not easy to learn. It takes years to develop."

"Everyone has aura, Gene. Even you."

"Auras, energy, Might, I've heard these terms."

"I think the Chasers were tracking your signature," she said softly. Gene's eyebrows shot up.

"What?"

"Your aura is green. Right now, you must be using it or something because it pulses around you. In this room," she gestured around her, "that color lingers, since you have used your ability." Gene's mouth hung open.

"Me? I don't have ability." Eva nodded her head. "No, you must be mistaken."

"If you believe that I can kill people, without even touching them, then can you believe me when I say you have the Might?" His eyes showed weariness, she could tell that this information was new to him. He was shaking his head still in denial. "If you want to keep the Chasers away, you can't walk your parameter and use your ability."

"I don't even know what it is! How can I use something that I didn't know I had?"

"Maybe it's when you are thinking, making plans? It must be something you do instinctual. Do you walk around thinking about your missions?"

"Sometimes."

"Then you're putting out a Might signature when you do so." He still looked as if he was unsure. Eva stood and approached him, placing a hand on his arm. He looked down at her, his green eyes still trying to figure her out. "I'm not trying to scare you. I'm just giving you the information I know. Yes, I did kill those guards, and the Chasers. And I was put in the tower because I've done it before, to Brosch's cronies." He nodded his head slowly.

Eva felt worry through her connection with Jace. He was looking for her and had not found her right away. He was ready to leave, which she was thankful for.

"I'll keep your secret Gene," she whispered. "Just like you'll keep mine."

"You're very complex, you know that Eva?" a shaky smile graced his lips.

"Just, stay inside Gene when you're planning and scheming. That should keep the Chasers off you." She let go of his arm and moved toward her pack. She lifted it and slung it over her shoulder. Her connection was strengthening, meaning that Jace was near.

She started toward the doors and turned back just before exiting. "I'm glad I was able to return the favor. Thanks again for your hospitality." Without hearing his response, she walked into the entryway where Jace was standing.

It was time to go look for more answers. She just hoped she didn't have to resort to extraction when they found who they were looking for.

Chapter 38
The Journey

Jace let Eva lead, since she supposedly knew the way. They left out of the same gate they entered, moving south. The first juncture they came to she turned west.

They rode in silence for a while, both probably trying to figure out this new connection between them. At least, that was what he was doing.

Before they left, Jace thanked Newly for his generosity in providing them food and a warm place to sleep. He could tell that Newly was tense and he kept giving Eva looks. He still wondered what that was all about. All he felt through his connection with Eva was that she was worried but also excited. Excited about what? Did Eva like Newly?

"Um, is that jealousy I'm feeling?" Eva's voice broke into his tumbling thoughts.

"Ah, no." Her eyebrow quirked and a small smile tugged at her lips. "Fine, it is."

"What do you have to be jealous about? Do you not want me to lead?"

"What? No. I'm fine with you leading. I was just thinking."

"I've been thinking too, but not something that would cause me to be jealous, so I figured I was feeling it from you."

"That's another thing. What is going on? How are we connected? I mean, I don't even have to touch you." That probably was the best part of the connection before this happened. Now he had no reason to touch her, and he very painfully wanted to.

When he woke that morning, he reached for her, but found nothing but air. He knew she was fine through the connection, but he still wanted to snuggle her. Oh Fates, he was close to breaking.

"I'm not sure," she answered from her seat on her horse. "I just know that I was, I don't know, sinking into these awful images and thoughts and I was pulled back out of them. When I opened my eyes, you were there," she glanced over at him with a relieved smile on her face. "I felt saved."

"Yeah, I was pretty determined not to lose you. I don't know what I did but I do remember some weird feelings, like I was reaching for you. And I felt when we, I don't know, connected. I wonder if that's what caused it."

"Maybe," she shrugged, not really knowing either. They were both in the dark on this one. He had never heard of it and if he had never heard of it, it's a good chance she hadn't heard about this either.

"Where are we headed? I meant to ask you a while ago."

"Southwest."

"Are you sure?" He reached into his breast pocket and pulled out the compass that Eva gifted to him on their birthday. He checked the dial, and it settled showing they were currently traveling west. When getting the gift, he used her braid of hair for the chain. Just looking at the two gifts that he received from Eva made him smile.

"Yes. Why, what is southwest from here?"

"Well," Jace tried picturing a map in his head as he placed the compass back in his pocket. "By the turns we've taken so far, we'll probably be heading back south again soon, correct?"

"Yes," she nodded.

"Then you're leading us to the Wedset Mountains."

"Yes, the mountain range," she was saying to herself. "That has to be it."

"Care to elaborate?"

"The vision I received showed me a mountain range beneath a particular constellation. Last night, I was checking to see where that constellation was, and I found it, southwest."

"That's why you were up there." He wondered why he found her on the roof. He got the sense that wasn't all that happened up there. "But I feel that wasn't the only thing that happened."

"Yeah, you're right," he could feel her resignation. She was silent for a few minutes. He could feel that she wasn't going to readily share.

"You can tell me later." He felt her gratitude. Jace knew that she had a hard time with explaining what she did and what she was capable of. She was a Seer; of that he was certain. But it was the other little things, like her weird pulse thing that could fling him backwards and the whole dropping Devon to his knees without touching him was still a mystery. He brought Nanna's journal along and he hoped to have time on this journey to maybe find some of those answers.

He hadn't found his answers yet, since the journal starts off with Nanna's first visions, when she was a teen. To say the least, it helped him understand his Nanna better by reading about her past life.

"Can you tell me about the mountains?" Eva asked.

"What would you like to know?"

"The name is familiar. Had I heard it before?"

"Wedset. Well, you know of the Wedset Lake just north of Jebrow Stronghold?" She nodded her head. "Well, it sits at the base of the Wedset Mountains on the south side. Where we are riding to is the north side of the mountains."

"And what's on this side?"

"Nothing." It was a desolate place. There was a brutal battle there during the Great War and most people avoided the mountains because of it. He didn't want to tell her that this little trip might not be fruitful.

"Ah, I remember now," he saw that familiar twinkle in her eye when she solved some puzzle. "Your father mentioned something about the mountain people of Wedset when he gave you the dagger."

"Oh yeah, he did."

"So, people used to live in the mountains?"

"A long time ago. It's probably been centuries now. The dagger has been in the family many generations. I do know that the mountain people were master craftsman of iron. Their weapons were the strongest, forged in the mountains. It was a great honor for my ancestor to receive such an item from the mountain people."

"What happened to them?"

"I'm not sure. All I can remember from my studies is that they were wiped out during one of the many invasions Hockland was experiencing at the time. You'd think with all that weaponry that they could fend their attackers off, but who knows what really happened. They are long dead now."

As Jace sat there on his horse, a weird feeling crept into his chest. He pressed his palm against it to distinguish what he was feeling. His face pulled down and he rolled his shoulders. It felt soul crushing. It was some deep sorrow. He looked over at Eva to ask if she felt it too when he realized her gaze was unfocused and she started to list to the side.

"Eva?" He moved his horse close to hers and shot out a hand to steady her. That's when he noticed her eyes were stark white. She was having a vision, one that was causing her pain, because now he realized that he was feeling that sorrow from their connection.

He grabbed her reigns and stopped her horse next to his. He was worried that she might fall so he got down and lifted her off her horse. He stood there holding her up like a doll in his arms. Her brow was furrowed, and she was slightly shaking. Tears leaked out of the corner of her eyes as the pain in his chest almost became unbearable. It was like his heart was breaking. He just held her to him, hoping that his embrace would show her through her vision that she was safe.

A few moments later her eyelids fluttered, and she focused right on him. The sorrow eased away into concern and a small sense of wonder.

"What is it?" he asked her.

"Can, can Seers see into the past?" Eva asked shakily.

"Um, I'm not sure." He had to get to reading Nanna's journal. So far Nanna hadn't written anything about that, but he wouldn't put it past him. He brushed a stray strand of her hair off her forehead, and he felt warmth spread in his chest. With his arms wrapped around he knew he was giving her the feeling of safety. But he also felt that flicker of desire.

Oh damnation, he was in trouble. He glanced down at her lips, slightly parted as her eyes drifted down to his lips as well. The feeling was double strength since she also was feeling the same. This connection was going to drive him nuts. This wasn't the time, with them standing in the middle of a well-traveled road. It was hard, but he restrained from the temptation, and he slowly stepped away from her. His hands were still on her shoulders since he wasn't sure if she was good to stand.

"You good?" he asked. She blinked several times and her brow scrunched. He felt a hint of confusion through the link, but she seemed to be alright.

"Yeah." He regretfully released her arms and turned to gather his horse.

"Do you want to rest?" he asked over his shoulder.

"No, I'm fine to continue," she grabbed her horse's reigns and patted the neck of her mare affectionately. "Can we walk for a while? I think I'd like to stretch my legs."

"Sure." They both started at a nice pace, walking with the horses at their side. He let her think for a bit because her emotions seemed to be all over the place. He was curious though, and he was sure she felt him the way he felt her.

"So, what was your vision about?"

"Well, some of it wasn't a vision."

"Okay, then what was it? You know that I felt something through the connection." Her head dropped slightly, and she sighed.

"Memories."

"From the feel of it, pretty bad ones?"

"Yeah, memories I thought I buried."

"Of your past?"

"Yeah. I was fine there at the start. It was showing me a vision, but it was like the toll for looking at it was seeing through my own past. I didn't like it." He knew that she was still struggling with that pain, just her thinking about it was making her sad.

"You don't have to tell me about your past, just the vision."

"Did you know that the mountain people lived in the mountains?"

"I only knew about them mining for the iron in the mountains. I thought all their settlements were at the base of the mountain." Eva shook her head slowly and a smile crept on her face.

"They created passageways inside the mountain. It's a maze of caves." A slow smile appeared on his face as well. What better way to hide then inside the mountains?

"There are people hiding in the mountains, right now." She nodded her head enthusiastically. "Well, if they aren't the mountain people, who could they be?"

"We'll find out when we get there." They certainly would. Maybe having Eva along wasn't so bad after all. Without her, he would have been stuck trying to convince Newly to give up the Rens location. Turns out, all he needed was a Seer to guide him.

Chapter 39
Can't Heal

"In here." Willow was directed by one of the Elites in the group to a small cave opening close to the main entrance. She had been deemed the Rens leader for the last ten years. Willow was the last known Seer that hadn't been either killed or captured by Brosch. Her visions had saved the Rens many times from capture. The group consisted of people with high ability and that included a large majority with the Might.

On most issues, she was consulted on what decision to make because they believed she had insight due to her ability. In the beginning she made all the decisions, but it was a heavy burden and at times it was difficult for her to decide, that's why she elected some other Ren members to make decisions for her on certain matters. Apparently, this matter was too great for one of them to decide alone what action to take.

As she strode into the room, she could feel the tension in the air. Another Elite lay on a thin mattress, clutching his side, his blue aura fluctuating. Two women who had talents in herbs and wounds were assessing the man, but they were not Might. They could only do so much for the man. A red angry slash showed across his middle. The Elite had sustained an injury and by the look on the women's faces, it didn't look good.

Ruby, her second-in-command, stepped up to her side. Her deep red aura pulsed around her. It seemed like the Seeker always had a permanent scowl on her face. "What's his status?" Willow asked.

"Not good," Ruby answered. "He was slashed across the stomach with a sword. It's not a deep wound however, it appears that the sword was stained."

"Poison," Willow shook her head slightly. Only one group of people would stain their weapons, Brosch's cronies. She approached the young man and could see the pain etched across his features. The women tending to him began removing his clothing to look at the wound.

Willow saw the lines of black slowly making their way out of the wound, confirmation that the poison was beginning to spread.

She bent down placing a calming hand on the man's shoulder. The Elite locked eyes with her and she saw his pleading look. What this man needed was a Healer. She turned slightly back and looked at Ruby. "Go retrieve the Numbered." Ruby gave her a swift nod and left the room. She turned back to the women who were now cleansing the wound.

"How long?" Willow asked.

"With the amount of spreading, he has two hours maybe," one woman answered with a solemn expression. Willow gently squeezed the man's shoulder and tried to give him an encouraging look. A few moments later, Ruby returned with their prisoner.

Willow stood and turned her gaze on the man. Based on the orange aura that pulsed around him, he was a Healer, and he better be a good one if Brosch kept him around. "Bring him closer," she instructed. Ruby pushed him forward where he stumbled slightly but got his feet under him to walk toward Willow.

"Numbered. You have been called upon for your ability." She stood aside so he could see the Elite that was on the thin mattress. The Numbered's eyes grew large at the sight of the injured man. He started to shake his head back and forth.

Willow narrowed her eyes at him. "This is where you either help on your own accord or you are forced to help. Depending on which will tell me who you are loyal to." The red-haired man tentatively stepped forward and knelt beside the Elite. She could see his pulsing aura and knew that he had the ability to heal him.

He held out his hands to the man and they were shaking. His brow started to sweat as he placed his hands near the man's wound. Willow saw him close his eyes and his brow scrunched. After a few moments he shook his head. "I can't," he barely was audible.

"What?" Ruby asked stepping menacingly close to his side. He opened his eyes, strain evident in the corners.

"I can't," he repeated. Ruby grabbed him by his shirt front and hefted him off his feet and glared at him, her aura reaching around him.

"What do you mean you can't? Is it because you still hold allegiance to Brosch? Is that it?" Ruby was practically screaming in his face.

"Ruby," Willow gently said. "Let him go." She could tell that Ruby didn't want to. "Ruby," she said with a little more authority. Ruby slowly released her death grip on his shirt and then finally dropped her hands at her side. She still gave him a death glare. It was Willow's turn.

She reached out with her ability and let it creep into him. Besides her Seer ability, she also had another rare ability. She was a Manipulator. She could convince others to do as she wanted. It was essentially mind control. In a calm voice she said to the Numbered, "You are going to heal this man because you want to help him. You do not want him to die."

Willow watched as the Numbered turned toward the Elite and looked down. Then it happened again. It was like her control started to slip so she pumped more influence toward him. When she had asked him about Brosch before, it was like this mental block where he couldn't tell her anything to do with the tyrant.

She could see his face started to show an underlying pain. In a strained voice he said, "I truly want to, but I," he stopped. Willow eased up and released him. He took a shuddering breath. How was it possible? His ability was blocked. He couldn't use it and she couldn't make him use it.

"Warren," she called to her head Elitist. His tall frame stood next to her. "Take the Numbered back to his cave. He is of no use to us." Warren nodded and grabbed the Numbered by his arm and led him out of the room. That was a puzzle to be sure. What kind of person did Brosch find that could block ability? It was unheard of.

Willow bent back down to the injured Elite. "Where did you run into the man who attacked you?" she asked gently.

"I was patrolling near the tower ruins," he said through clenched teeth. "I was jumped when I reached the large boulders coming back." He sucked in a shuddering breath and continued, "I got his arm and thinking I was the victor was not expecting his attack. He ran off before I could deal the final blow." He gritted his teeth and groaned as one of the women poured a liquid on the wound that made it sizzle. "I failed you."

"No, you cannot blame yourself," Willow reassured him. "You have fought bravely and have served the Rens faithfully. Believe in that. Rest and let these women take care of you." She rose to her feet, knowing this man in a few hours would join the afterlife. There was no cure for the poison.

She turned away from him and started walking out the cave's entrance. Ruby saddled up to her side. "What's the plan?"

"Call for a meeting. We have been found and very soon we will be visited by a Brosch army." They had been in these caves too long. They should have moved on to a new location, except her vision showed two people were coming. She knew the Rens had to stay and wait for them, even with the risk of exposure.

"Can we not just escape?" Ruby roughly asked.

"No. By the time we pack up and head out, they will be waiting for us. We will stand and fight. Planning the battle to our advantage is the only way we will make it out alive." The Rens were large in number, but not as large as a Brosch army. Willow knew they would be outnumbered. They needed a little finesse. This group had the brightest minds around, she was sure of it. "Have everyone convene in the large cavern, immediately."

"Right away," Ruby said and peeled away down another corridor to gather the troops. Willow continued thinking about her vision. Two large shapes came on foot, holding weapons, each coming for a different purpose, one seeking a Seer and the other seeking the Numbered. She couldn't identify the people. The vision appeared just as quickly as it was gone, too quickly for her to take in any details.

She also believed that one of these two people was the Child. The Numbered said that he was seeking the One, the renowned Child of the prophesy. It was not a coincidence that the Numbered ended up with the Rens. It was fate to bring the One who would overthrow Brosch to the people who despised him the most, the people of Might.

Willow sure hoped she was getting warriors because the Rens needed all the help they could get.

Chapter 40
Battle

"Hold." Jace reigned in, stopping his horse. They were closing in on the edge of the mountains. He was getting an uneasy feeling, especially being exposed on the road. Eva stopped beside him, looking at him with a questioning look. She could probably feel what his emotions were, because hers changed right along with his.

He silently motioned for them to dismount. He led his horse into the dense grouping of trees that lined the base of the mountain. Once he and Eva were clear of the road, he took out some treats and grain and sprinkled them on the ground. Both horses moved toward the food and began munching. He didn't want to tie them up, just in case if anything happened to them, the horses at least could have a chance to fend for themselves.

Jace unlaced his sword from his mount and strapped it to his back, along with a bow and quiver of arrows. He saw Eva out of the corner of his eye gather her weapons as well. He tucked the family dagger into the back of his waistband. He walked over to Eva, waiting for her to finish. "We'll continue on foot," he said in a low voice.

She nodded her head. They both walked silently through the trees, treading lightly. The sky was overcast so their movements were hidden better than if light streamed through the trees. They didn't have to worry about avoiding the light when there wasn't any light to avoid.

A half hour later, Jace directed their path back toward the road. As they came close, he found a large bush that could easily hide both Eva and him. He crouched behind it, scanning the road beyond.

"What is that?" Eva whispered at his side, pointing at some ruins just up the way.

"An old watchtower I'm guessing. Probably like the one you were found in," he whispered back. He felt a slight emotion of anger through their connection. Obviously, that was something he shouldn't bring up.

"Why are we waiting here?"

"There's something coming. I can feel it." It was hard to explain, but he felt these vibrations. He didn't know how he knew. He just knew that it meant something was close by. It was like the ground was vibrating from the pounding it was receiving.

"Are you sure?"

"As sure as you are about your visions." She nodded her head in understanding, because they both knew visions were prickly. Just because he had a feeling didn't mean it was right, but it was better to play it safe.

Jace scanned up and down the road, not picking up anything out of the ordinary. It was slightly eerie though. The clouds created shadows that he swore people could be lurking in. He was anxious and he could feel that his anxiety was causing Eva to become anxious as well. He needed to keep it under control. The only way to handle any situation was to be calm.

Several minutes passed and down the road something loomed. It grew large and was as wide as the road. It took him a moment, but he realized what he was seeing. It was people. Not just any people though. He saw few on horseback and the majority were walking. There were hundreds of them. The closer they came the more he could see them.

"Cronies," Jace heard Eva hiss out beside him.

"Brosch's? How do you know?" he whispered back.

"It's their auras. I would know it anywhere."

"What about them?" He hadn't realized that Eva could see auras. It sounded odd to him that she could tell that they were associated with Brosch. If he recalled from his Nanna so many years ago, everyone had their own unique aura and color, although similar, rarely were colors the same.

"The color isn't as bright. It's like the color is tainted, like it's dull."

"That could be anyone," he said disbelieving. She turned her eyes toward him, her gaze steady with his. She grabbed his hand, which he didn't know why.

"Look again," she said as she glanced toward them.

"Okay, what am I looking at?"

"See around them. Auras outline a person. Just feel what I'm feeling and use that to see them."

He glanced down at their fingers that were wound with each other, and he did start to feel something through their hands. It wasn't like the connection they had before when their skin met, but it was something that he could focus on. He breathed out and looked up at the coming hoard again, this time really focusing around each person.

He gasped, surprised that he was seeing something he possibly couldn't be. He blinked several times, but it was still there. Each person had a color that emanated from them. Most color was blue, but Eva was right, it was very dull, like seeing the color through a filter.

Jace caught her look back at him with a slight smile on her face. He matched her smile and shook his head side to side. "Is that what you see all the time?" he asked in awe.

"Auras, yes. That specific color, no." Her face grew serious, and she released their hands to grip the hilt of her sword. "That color is evil. They are not our allies." He could feel through their link her anger rising. She associated that aura with the enemy. He knew that she had been captured by Brosch and she had interactions with his cronies. It would make sense that when she saw that aura, she wanted vengeance.

"The question is, what are his cronies doing here?" He couldn't believe that Brosch would send this large number if it wasn't for a reason. Eva was so worked up over seeing them, she wasn't paying attention. That would be bad if they had to fight them. "Eva, you need to remain calm. Feel my emotions. Its fine to be angry, but your emotions need to remain in check. You'll do something stupid if you don't have a clear head." He placed a reassuring hand on her shoulder. He felt the tension slowly release until he could feel with their connection that she was in control. He squeezed her shoulder and brought his hand back to his side.

When she turned, she gave Jace a grateful look. But then her eyes looked passed him and he saw her blink a few times. He turned his head in the direction she was looking and caught what she was seeing.

There were people creeping through the forest and some started to move out to the road. Strange, since Eva showed him the aura thing, he could see it without having to hold her hand. What he saw was completely different than the hoard coming down the road.

"Who are they?" he asked.

"I don't know." He smirked and gave her a sidelong look.

"I thought you knew everybody Eva."

"Don't be ridiculous Jace. Only Brosch's cronies have that distinct aura. These ones, they're," she paused, and she shook her head.

"Awesome?" he offered. A smile spread across her face.

"Normal. That's what auras are supposed to look like." He looked back at the people that were slowly gathering in their own group to face off with Brosch's cronies.

"They're so bright."

"Looks like that's why Brosch's cronies are here," she determined. He couldn't agree more. At their vantage point, they were going to be seeing the action happen right in front of them.

Tension rode high in the air from the opposing forces. The hoard stopped on the road, now spanning out to the sides, taking up as much space to stop any attempted escape. The other group stood strong together, holding their weapons readying for what was to come next.

On cue, arrows soared through the overcast sky, hurtling toward the people that came out of the mountains. He watched as each one either blocked or swatted the arrow away before it pierced them. Looking back and forth between the groups, he could tell that the Brosch hoard was much larger compared to the other. And that hoard roared and started to charge.

The other group took off as well, intent on meeting them in the middle. At the first clash of swords, he watched as the two groups of men beat on each other. Brosch's cronies were no slouches. They were trained and tough.

Jace's heart was racing. It was hard to keep hidden while a battle was going on. Something sang in his blood and his hands began to twitch with excitement. This wasn't their fight. Suddenly, Eva took off beyond their cover toward the fight raising her weapon.

"Eva!" he shouted at her. He withdrew his bow and notched an arrow and took off after her. She wasn't going to die on his watch.

She couldn't take it anymore. These people needed help. Brosch's cronies were intent on slaughtering them all. Eva raced toward the fray, not caring that she had left the safety of the brush. It would be cowardly to watch these men die when she was more than capable of helping them.

A sword came down toward a brightly colored aura's back as he was fighting another crony. Eva was just fast enough to block the crony's sword. She pushed him away and before she could kill him, an arrow protruded from his front. She whipped her head around and saw Jace.

She watched as he notched another arrow and released in another direction, felling another crony. He looked glorious, muscles flexing from the tension in his bow and his form larger than most anyone on the field. He looked like a god. There was no time to think about that. There were more cronies to take down. She just hoped that Jace didn't steal any more of her opponents.

Another charged toward her, and she was able to block the massive blow. It was a little jarring, but she was able to use his momentum to spin around him. He lost sight of her and that's when she made her strike. Her sword sunk into his chest. As she pulled it back to her the man sunk to his knees and collapsed on the ground.

She'd thought that killing would affect her, but it didn't. This was different than what she did before. Although she knew his Spark would be leaving him soon, it was for the best. He was corrupt. She turned just in time to block a sword swinging down toward her.

Eva stepped forward instead of back, catching the man off guard and she sunk her dagger into the man's neck. The look of surprise in his face fueled her on. She took on two other opponents, blocking and paring. Her movements were fluid, and she was able to avoid each strike and felled both, one with a sword through his middle and the other her dagger sticking out of his neck where she threw it.

She retrieved her dagger quickly and moved on to help another bright-aura solider. When she felled the crony the solider that she saved turned and looked at her in surprise. He was probably trying to determine if she was the enemy, but it's not like he had any time to decide.

She ran off to another solider that was being attacked. Eva felt invigorated. She was gaining attention though. As she was fighting off two cronies, three more sprinted toward her. Instinctively she sent out her pulse, which pushed all the men surrounding her away. They were sprawled on their backs from shock.

Two of them she was able to kill before the others got up. She threw her dagger, killing one other and then she was finally down to a manageable number again. After blocking and moving out and around the men several times, she was able to fell both.

As Eva drove her sword into the crony a sharp pain radiated from her middle. She cried out and looked down. But she was not injured. Her head jerked around and caught sight of the only man with no aura, blood seeping out of his stomach.

"Jace!" she cried out. Something broke inside her. Seeing the man that she was so closely tied with hurt sent her into a place that she had never been before. All she could think about was getting to him and protecting him.

She raced toward him, retrieving her dagger as she went. He watched Jace fall to his knees, and she felt the pain along their connection. Jace didn't see the man that prowled toward him, his sword raised above his head to give Jace a deathly blow.

She reached out with her thread toward the crony and thought of ripping out his heart. What she realized she did was what she did to the men outside Newly's Stronghold. She took his Spark. The man dropped dead before he even reached Jace.

Eva finally reached Jace's side. She stood in front of him and looked around, prepared to take on the whole of Brosch's army to keep him safe.

"Eva? What are you doing? Get out of here! Get to safety!" she heard Jace say. He was still in pain, but he was determined, rising behind her.

Before she could say anything, they were charged by two of Brosch's cronies. They fought side by side, both taking out their opponents. A large group of them started to charge toward them. She directed her pulse toward the men in front of her and they flew backward. She reached with her thread and ripped the Sparks out of the men on her right and she raised her sword to fight the others. As she was fighting, she was very aware of Jace's position. If she saw a crony almost get him, she would yank the crony's Spark and he would drop.

She continued to fight, killing any crony close enough to her with her weapons and any that seemed to think they would sneak up on either her or Jace were stripped of their Spark. Through the connection she could still feel Jace's pain, even though he was fighting through it, still taking out Brosch's cronies.

She fell one after another, only knowing one thing. She had to kill these evil men for what they did to her and for threatening the only person see cared about.

Jace's strength was weakening. The cut wasn't deep, but it was like it was draining him of his energy anyway. He blocked and parried and cut and slashed. With each blow he could feel his arms growing tired. His body wanted to sleep, but Eva was his primary focus.

Seeing her in battle was an amazing sight. He knew that she could take care of herself, but he was still afraid for her life. He didn't want anything to happen to her. As if admitting now, in the heat of battle, that he was starting to have feelings for her, was a bit of an understatement.

He dropped to one knee and a looming figure appeared in his blurred vision. He raised his sword, but the blow never came. The man dropped down in front of him, eyes wide, as if shocked to death. Jace realized he was no good. His sword tumbled out of his fingers toward the ground. It was like his limbs were giving up.

Jace fell to the side, landing in the blood-soaked grass. A cut shouldn't hurt this bad. Something was wrong. Through his connection with Eva, he felt an icy cold rage. He was startled by how consuming her feeling was. He saw through the blur her long hair above him. She was defending him. He forced his vision to clear up to see around him.

Eva's chest heaved up and down from exertion and when she glanced down at him, his breath caught a little in his throat. Her eyes were pitch black. That wasn't normal. But with a blink, her eyes shone their usual hazel color, and her feelings changed from rage to worry.

She dropped to her knees at his side running her hands all over him. She stopped when she reached his stomach, where he knew an angry red line appeared. She inhaled sharply as her eyes grew wide at the wound.

"It's nothing," he rasped. "I'm fine." Droplets of rain began to fall.

"You're in pain," she said with a wavering voice. Tears were starting to form at the corners of her eyes, mixing with the rain.

"Nah, it's nothing," even though as he said that he winced. It was like the pain had reached out to his nerve endings. Instead of feeling any more sadness from her, he felt determination.

Eva placed her hands on either side of his wound and stared down with a scrunched brow. It was only a second, when he felt a sensation spread throughout his body. It grabbed on to each place he could feel the pain. Then, it was like the pain was being drawn out of him, except he was feeling it somewhere else.

Pain shot through the link. He didn't know what Eva was doing, but she needed to stop. She shouldn't be in pain. He tried to draw the pain away like he did before. He reached up and placed a hand on her cheek. A rush of pain shot through him and down into a cavern inside him. The sensation stopped abruptly and so did the pain. Only a lingering ache in his body and through their connection remained.

Her eyes drifted toward his and their gazes locked. She threw her arms around him, and he could feel her relief. He brought his arms securely around her, thankful that she was safe. He was not okay with her putting her life in danger. She moved back to allow him to sit up. As he did, he looked down and saw that the wound he had was gone. That's impossible. He reached down and only the rain which was washing his blood away was on his skin.

Jace gazed up at Eva in awe. Was she? "Are you a Healer?" he croaked out. A smile quirked at the corners of her mouth.

"Maybe," she shrugged.

"I think this is more than a maybe."

"Okay, so I might also have healing ability."

"How did you know?"

"I've always had it," she stated matter-of-factly.

"And you didn't tell me?"

"Was I supposed to?"

"Yes, of course you should have." She looked at him apologetically. He wasn't mad at her, it just changed everything. Eva was different. It was like she had more than one ability. Was that even possible? He had never heard of such a thing.

"Here, let's get you to your feet," she said and started to help him up. Not like he needed it, since he no longer felt weak. As they stood, they noticed they were surrounded by the bright-aura people. They must have created the circle around them when she was healing him.

"Great, now what?" he said out of the corner of his mouth. He didn't like the assessing stares he was getting from these men. He knew none of them had his strength. If he didn't have more than three on him at a time, he could make it out ahead.

The circle parted and his gaze turned to a cloaked figure entering the circle. An interesting violet color aura shimmered around the figure. The hood fell away from the cloak to show an older woman with white hair and pale blue eyes. Jace's own eyes widen. Pale-colored eyes. His Nanna had pale-colored eyes, because of the many times in her life that she saw visions. The woman standing in front of them was a Seer. He concluded these people must be the Rens.

"Jace?" Eva asked at his side. His arm was still protective around her. Through the connection he suddenly felt what she was feeling. He looked at her and saw her eyes drooping. She was tired, probably from fighting and using her abilities. "I'm tired," she breathed out.

He felt her legs go and he held her to his chest. He wasn't concerned with any of the stares around him, she needed a place to rest, and they were either going to help him or kill him. He scooped her up in his arms and cradled her to his chest. Her breathing was even and through the connection she was calm and safe.

He reluctantly moved his gaze from her face to the Seer. There was no time for pleasantries. "We are not here to hurt any of you," he said. "We did not travel all this way to be involved in a fight."

"I know," the Seer said. Of course, she probably predicted their arrival. He watched as she motioned behind her. Two men stepped forward. "These men will escort you to our shelter. Of course, we will be preparing to leave, since our location has been compromised." He noticed that the men tightened their holds on their sheathed swords.

The Seer didn't trust them. Well, would he trust a stranger that helped him fight off the enemy? No, he probably would need to learn more about the person. So, they were to be escorted by armed men. It was like they were prisoners. Better alive and in the hands of the Rens than dead or in the hands of Brosch.

"We'll provide you a meal and place to rest for your services. I will send someone to look at your friend," the Seer pointed at Eva's prone form in his arms.

"No need. She is just sleeping."

"Very well." The Seer raised her hood against the rain and turned on her heel. The men pressed close to his back. Obviously, he was meant to follow her. He followed the Seer back toward the mountains.

Jace didn't know what was in store for him and Eva. He found the Seer he was looking for. That means he was with the Rens. His questions might finally be answered. His Nanna had only one prophesy in her life. He envisioned the words in his mind that he read from her journal.

The Child has been born. The Mighty has been born. Only the Child can merge and become One. Child and Mighty. Light and dark, equal. The One will bring balance. Guided by the Fates, the One will save us all.

His Nanna prophesied mere moments after his birth. His Nanna died believing that he was the Child. Jace's question for the Seer, was he the Child prophesy?

Epilogue

"Enter," he said sitting behind his massive desk where he currently was going over the stronghold reports, lightning flashed against the window as a storm beat against his home. Rudd had required payment from each stronghold, otherwise he would just take what resources he wanted along with some of their children. What people will give you when you threaten their families, he smirked at the thought.

A small man entered, one with fear in his eyes. He approached Rudd's desk and fell to his knees and bowed before him. The man was trembling.

"Sir," the man's voice shook. His clothes dripped water onto the floor. The man obviously had just come from outside. "I have news from the effort." Yes, just what Rudd was waiting for. His dark brown eyes bore into the top of the man's head. He stood from his seat and came around to the sniveling man.

"And what news is that?"

"We have been defeated."

"What?!" Rudd yelled. His army, defeated? That was impossible. He had the strongest in the land. No one can oppose him and his forces.

"It seemed that we underestimated them," the man's voice was squeaky with uncertainty, as he should be.

"Stand up," Rudd growled. The small man rose and trembled where he stood. He looked pathetic. The rain made him look like a drenched rat. He approached the man, inches from his face. "Tell me what you saw."

"It wasn't anything I've ever seen. We outnumbered them, but they had some unknown force on their side."

"Unknown force?"

"I saw soldiers drop on their own, faces pulled in open horror. Dead before they even hit the ground." Rudd's mind sparked from an old memory. How many years had it been? He turned away from the man and a slow sardonic smile appeared on his face. There was only one person he knew of that could kill like that.

"You did nothing to help your fellow soldiers? You ran for your life?" He pushed his ability toward the man, making him lift his dagger out of his belt. The man tried to resist, but it was futile.

"Please no. I beg forgiveness. I thought it was only right to let you know this information as soon as possible." He released the hold on the man, and he could hear him sigh audibly.

"Yes, I do appreciate the information." Rudd turned quickly catching the man off guard and slashed his throat open with the dagger he had hidden in his sleeve. He watched the man gurgle, clamping his hands around his neck. His shocked expression was clear on his face as the men fell to the floor, bleeding out from the wound, blood mixing with the rainwater. He could have had the man kill himself, but he felt much better doing it with his own hand. It was a good stress reliever.

"Onyx!" he called his guard forward. The large mountain of a man stood at his side. "I need an expert Tracker. Bring me 015." Onyx nodded and strode to the door. "And get someone in here to clean this mess up," he called after him.

Rudd moved back to his chair and sank down in. He found her. After all these years, she messed-up and exposed herself. Was she with the Rens this whole time? He should have pressed harder to find these wretched people if he had any inclination that she was there. How long has it been? Seven years? His eyes twinkled with the knowledge of retrieving his most prized possession.

His study door opened a minute later, Onyx returned with 015 and a few lowly servants. The servants shuffled in and went to work with removing the now dead man at front of his desk. 015 approached and stood tall, looking at Rudd with black eyes. Any normal person would run in fear in the other direction, but Rudd created this man to be who he was.

"015. I have a job for you. We have located stolen property and I'm afraid the Chasers will not be enough to bring this Numbered to me."

"As you see fit, sir," he bowed his head. 015's contrasting white-blonde hair made his dark eyes stand out even more. But he trusted this man to do his job. 015 knew the consequences of disobeying an order.

"Bring me 1 and you'll be rewarded." The man before him only raised one eyebrow at the task, his surprised face. "She's currently holed up in the Wedset Mountains. Find her and bring her back."

"It will be done, Brosch," 015 nodded his head and immediately turned on his heel and left.

Rudd grinned manically. She was the first child he ever took. She had potential, even at such a young age, all that raw ability in such a small package. He had never seen anyone of her equal.

Very soon he'd have her back. No one will dare oppose him with her under his thumb. He laughed at the prospect of a world rid of the Might. He will snuff out every living being with it, only keeping the best for himself of course.

He didn't believe in the Child prophesy and that they were all destined by the Fates. What a bunch of rubbish! He believed in making his own path, carving out his own destiny. Rudd Brosch was the only ruler that this country needed, and he would slaughter anyone who thought otherwise.

Author Biography

W.W. Morse is naturally a creative person. Creating stories and being able to share them has been an eventful journey. Morse lives in the Midwest and is happily married and has two adorable children. The family goes on many adventures together, especially to their cabin in the woods. They raise chickens and have one incredibly old cat named Bob. Morse is currently a quality analyst yet still finds time for family and working on other hobbies. Some hobbies include playing Horn, gardening, reading, bowling, and baking. Morse was always busy at an early age, and it's no different now. "I thank my parents who allowed me to buy all those books from scholastic book fair when I was younger. If I wasn't surrounded by books at a young age, I don't think I would be the writer I am today."

Stay connected with W.W. Morse

https://www.instagram.com/webmorse/

https://www.facebook.com/w.w.morse

Becoming One
Book 2 in Might Series coming Spring 2023!